The Misenberg Accelerator

THOMAS NELSON PUBLISHERS
Nashville • Atlanta • London • Vancouver

Books in the
Perimeter One Adventures series

The Misenberg Accelerator (Book One)

The SHONN Project (Book Two)

Out of Time (Book Three)

The Mines of Venus (Book Four)

Published in Nashville, Tennessee, by Thomas Nelson, Inc., Publishers, and distributed in Canada by Word Communications, Ltd., Richmond, British Columbia.

Library of Congress Cataloging-in-Publication Data

Ward, David, 1961–
    The Misenberg Accelerator / David Ward.
        p.   cm.—(Perimeter One adventures series; bk. 1)
    Summary: When a symposium takes Dr. Graham to the Perimeter One space station at the edge of the solar system, sabotage places his entire family in terrible danger.
    ISBN 0-8407-9235-2 (hardcover)
    [1. Science fiction.]   I. Title.   II. Series: Ward, David, 1961–
Perimeter One adventures series; bk. 1.
PZ7.W1873M1   1994
[Fic]—dc20   94–10517
                                                                   CIP
                                                                    AC

Printed in the United States of America.

3 4 5 6 — 99 98 97 96

Prologue

The light in the secret cargo bay was dim, the air dank and musty. Old shipping containers lay scattered along one wall, discarded long ago. A door in the wall hissed open, and stagnant air billowed out into the hallway beyond. Light from the open door revealed the silhouette of a man as he stepped into the shadows of the cargo bay.

The door closed again, and the man stood very still for a moment, listening. He touched a panel by the door, and dim emergency lights came on along the edges of the ceiling. After a few seconds, the quiet was so thick he could hear his own heart beating. Without warning, there was a banshee wail of metal scraping on metal. The man jumped a bit, then covered his ears and strode over to the controls next to the bay doors. Slowly, and with much effort, the doors creaked open.

Inside lay the docking area of a small space ship, as dimly lit as the cargo bay. Three figures huddled a few paces inside. The figure in the middle stepped forward.

"Looks like we've come to the right place."

The man in the cargo bay tried to distinguish the face before him. "Welcome. Why all the secrecy?"

"It wouldn't do for me to be recognized by some overly eager security guard, now would it?"

"No, I suppose not. You said you had a plan."

The figure laughed unpleasantly. "Oh yes."

"What is it?"

"To bring horrified outrage to every journalist and politician in this solar system, and profound misery to Dr. Nathan Graham. . . ."

CHAPTER 1

 "Ryan!"

Millie Graham was in no mood to wait. Her son had retreated to his bedroom some fifteen minutes ago, and had not been heard from since. Ryan was a good kid, but he suffered from the abbreviated attention span that seems to afflict all fifteen-year-olds.

Amie walked up the short stairway from the kitchen, pulling a pair of white knit gloves over her delicate hands. Tonight was the last of the winter concerts at the junior high school, and she was supposed to provide piano accompaniment for several of her classmates. She was, understandably, a bit nervous about the whole thing, and her brother's insensitivity to the situation wasn't helping matters at all.

"Mom, we're going to be late!" Amie said impatiently.

"Ryan!"

Ryan's voice came muffled from behind his bedroom door. "I'll be right down."

Millie had heard that one before. Shaking her head, she hung her purse over the bannister and pounded up the stairs. Rounding the post at the top of the stairs, she made a beeline for her son's door. He jumped at her entrance but never took his eyes from the computer screen. At the moment, he had his hands full blasting alien spacecraft. The Zarkons were deter-

1

mined to take over the universe, and Ryan was the only thing standing in their way.

"I'm coming! Really! Just one more minute," Ryan pleaded.

Millie stood beside him, her arms crossed. "Your sister is going to shoot you. Now turn it off and let's go."

"Just thirty seconds! I'm about to beat my high score!"

The threat to the universe notwithstanding, Millie reached down and switched off her son's computer.

"AAAAGH!" Ryan wailed. "You couldn't wait another four hundred thousand points?"

"On your feet, space warrior. Don't forget your jacket. It's cold out."

Mother and son walked downstairs together, then she noticed his shoes. "Why aren't you wearing your boots?"

"I forgot. Besides, these are comfortable."

"You may not think so once we're outside," Millie retorted. In the entryway, Amie stood tapping her foot impatiently.

"You were playing *Plague of the Zarkons* again, weren't you?"

Ryan rolled his eyes. "Oh, relax. You act as if the whole world were coming just to see you play."

Amie pressed her lips together to keep from saying something nasty. "I'm supposed to help the choir warm up."

Ryan opened the door and was hit with a wall of frigid air from outside. "Whooo! Looks like they're going to need it."

The trip to the school proceeded in relative silence. The car seemed empty without their father. Amie knew he was very busy tying up loose ends in preparation for their upcoming trip to the Perimeter One Station at the edge of the solar system. *Oh, Lord,* she thought, *please help him make it to the concert.*

Amie arrived with only a couple of minutes to spare, and made it to the piano bench on stage just before the curtain went up. Her heart rose in her throat while the choir waited for the director's downbeat. This first piece was the one she had been dreading, the one she had never made it through without a mistake. Redoubling her concentration, she slowly drifted into that magical place where the whole world consisted only of her and the music. She existed only for the next note, the next measure, the next phrase, and sailed over the problem spot without even noticing.

Before she knew it, the piece was over and the crowd, many of them parents, burst into frantic applause. Amie breathed a sigh of relief. She had made it, and without a single mistake. Scanning the rows of faces for one in particular, she caught sight of her mother and Ryan in one of the lower sections on the left. Millie was grinning from ear to ear, clapping for all she was worth. And there in the aisle seat was her father.

The Grahams stopped for ice cream at their favorite little shop on the way home, even though the temperature outside was below freezing. Dessert was a celebrated tradition in their family, and no particular reason was required. Tonight, however, they had good reason. Amie's concert had been a resounding success, and their father had some important news to share with his family.

Dr. Nathan Graham was a tall, dark-haired man in his late forties, and there were few things he would allow to interfere with the enjoyment of ice cream. He sat working on a hot fudge sundae while his wife Millie, an attractive woman with dark hair nicely highlighted with gray, politely tucked into a strawberry chocolate chip ice cream cone. Ryan and Amie had both chosen ice cream bars, but their approaches were quite different. Ryan had eaten all the chocolate coating off his bar almost before the paper was removed, while Amie rationed out enough chocolate for every bite. With dessert behind them the family settled back in their chairs, ready to hear Nathan's news.

"The itinerary finally came in this evening. We're booked on a shuttle from Dulles to McKinley Launching Station on Thursday afternoon next week."

Ryan looked interested. "Where's McKinley Station?"

"In orbit."

Ryan had been on orbital stations before, but never McKinley. "Cool. They'll stick a shuttle on a jumbo transport and piggyback into the upper atmosphere, right?"

Nathan nodded. "It beats a vertical takeoff, believe me. The shuttle will be riding on the back of an old 787. We'll blast off when we reach sixty thousand feet."

Amie frowned. "Why go to all that trouble?"

Nathan took a drink of water from a paper cup. "It's much cheaper to launch an interplanetary ship from space. You use a lot less fuel."

"How long will we be in transit to the Perimeter One Station?" Millie asked.

"About three weeks. There won't be a lot to do on the ship, but the accommodations should be nice enough."

Millie smiled. "You couldn't find a nice symposium in Hawaii?"

Nathan laughed. "How many people do you know who have ever set foot on the Perimeter One Station?"

"Only one. I just don't know why you want to go back."

"As you well know, I was invited. Besides, I still think this is a super opportunity for the chilluns."

"Us chilluns think it's a pretty great idea, too," Ryan chimed in as Amie nodded.

Millie was not impressed. "You think anything that takes you out of school is a great idea. I just hope you stay caught up on your studies while we're gone."

"Don't worry. They heaped it on pretty good," Ryan replied, obviously none too happy about the prospect.

Millie caught her son's attention, a gentle warning in her eyes. "Your teachers did the same thing last time we took a trip, only you conveniently forgot your books. I assure you that won't happen this time."

Ryan tried to look outraged but failed hopelessly. "Mother! How could you think such a thing?"

*　*　*

In a world where the sun never shines, without atmosphere, without life, a shiny silver repair vehicle rolled slowly up a canyon. On either side stood a precipitous obsidian cliff, each marked at random intervals by gossamer threads of purest gold. Smaller geometric outcroppings of brightly colored metals were fused along the walls at regular intervals, which upon closer inspection seemed to be pulsing with energy.

"Plasma terminals are in good condition."

At the controls of the repair vehicle, Chris Graham was enthralled by the dim angular views all around, and found it difficult to maintain his regular verbal reports. There were no wind, clouds, or rain, and therefore no erosion, nor would there ever be, for this was a sterile world. The vehicle emerged from the canyon and started down into a wide valley, seemingly populated by an alien city. Glowing streets crisscrossed the valley as more complex geometric structures clustered asymmetrically across the landscape.

Chris turned his head to the left, and noticed one of the large, pulsing geometric structures nearby. Straight ahead, across the road from the vehicle, was a gargantuan, single-story structure, supported by long rows of tremendous metal legs.

"I'm at the secondary power conduit, facing the IL coprocessor. Which direction to the CPU cache channels?"

A voice came over the speaker in his helmet. "Turn left five-point-seven-three millimeters."

"That's a long drive. Any chance of getting fried?"

"All the submicron switches in your quadrant have been shut off. You should be free and clear to navigate."

Chris looked down at the control panel in front of him with the computer-generated image of his hands turning the steering handles. As the vehicle completed its turn, Chris thought the coprocessor looked even more immense from this angle, and he had to remind himself that the massive structure would actually fit on the head of a pin. The tiny vehicle he was controlling would be difficult to find, even with a microscope.

Physically, Chris was in a white room, empty except for the chair in which he sat and a simple control panel mounted in front of him. He was wearing a full body suit, interlaced with sensors so that his movements would be reflected on the monitor in his helmet. Unaware of his true surroundings, his only reality for the moment was the one generated by his belt-mounted computer, based on the input it was receiving from the repair vehicle.

This particular repair vehicle was a prototype microscopic remote vehicle, or MRV, used to fix computers and machinery. The computer Chris was currently repairing belonged to the biology department, and they were not keen on the idea of a nonbiology student wandering around inside one of their computers. Chris, however, was the one who had engineered this nifty little marriage between virtual reality and microscopic machinery, and this was one job that had to be done right.

The computers were manufactured in a vacuum to tolerances in excess of one thousand years between component failure. Exposure to atmosphere would destroy some of the more sensitive components, but the casings were hermetically sealed to prevent such an occurrence. In theory, these machines were maintenance free, but every now and then something unforeseen happened. Then the problem was how to repair them without causing further damage.

The MRV had been injected by hypodermic through the self-sealing membrane on one of the control panels on the front of the biology department's ailing computer. Chris had taken nearly six hours to maneuver his machine through the various layers to the main computer core where the problem was located. He was tired and stiff, but the thrill still hadn't worn off.

"I'm passing the cache channels now. All pathways appear nominal . . . hold it. Looks like your diagnostic was right. Number four is out."

"That shouldn't be possible."

"I'm going to check it out."

The tiny vehicle moved into a long, narrow canyon, which looked by scale to be several hundred feet high, but stood only a fraction of a millimeter above the surface of the circuit board. Chris was straining to see ahead, as the illumination from the vehicle's running lights was limited. Something caught his eye and he slowed to a stop just in time to avoid toppling into a pit.

"You've got some corrosion on the pathway. Scanning for source."

Chris looked around but found only the smooth surface of the cache channel. Turning his attention upward, he saw the problem immediately. At his direction, the repair vehicle climbed the wall using its adhesive wheels, and soon popped out on top. Chris surveyed the damage.

"Looks like there's acid on one of the anchor cleats. Tiny particles have been falling down into the cache channel. My guess is someone in quality control dropped the ball."

"Can you fix it?"

"The cleat's still in good shape. I'll need a second look at the corrosion down below before I can tell you."

Chris operated a different set of controls and a tiny laser extended from the front of the repair vehicle. Carefully targeting only the corroded portion of the cleat, he melted the exterior to secure any particles in place, then proceeded back down the wall to the bottom of the cache channel.

"The hole's pretty deep. I'll need additional material."

There was a long pause, while the people on the other end consulted their schematics. Chris didn't like the way the biology students hoarded their secrets, but he had to respect them just the same. These guys really knew their stuff.

"There's a terminated junction just past the entrance to the channel. The anterior portion is unnecessarily reinforced for high-impact usage. Take what you need."

The MRV motored back down the channel, turned left, and

stopped in front of a large black box with several hefty columns of metal securing it to the circuit board. Chris carved out a semicircular piece from one of the columns and used both sets of claws to pick it up. The size of the load made the MRV harder to maneuver, but he was able to compensate, and was soon back at the edge of the pit in the cache channel. He lowered the chunk of metal into the pit and activated the laser once more, fusing the sides of the pit to the new piece.

"I welded a patch in the corroded section. The channel should work now."

To his astonishment, a voice in the background said, "Power up."

"No! Wait! Give me a chance to. . . ."

There was a bright flash and the screen inside the helmet went dark. In the lower right corner, small green letters read NO INPUT.

Chris jerked the helmet off in frustration and set it down on the control panel. A door in the wall slid open, and Emmanuel Hascome walked in. Manny was Chris's roommate, best friend, and the one responsible for roping him into this in the first place.

Manny looked apologetic. "Sorry about that."

"Who gave the order to power up?"

"That was Darrell Webster. He's a grad student, and I'm afraid he doesn't think much about other people. You didn't really want to try to maneuver that thing out of there, did you?"

Chris was trying not to take his anger out on his friend. "I was willing to give it a shot."

"Did the MRV cost very much? We'd be happy to reimburse you."

"It's not the materials; it's the time. I had almost one hundred hours invested in that thing."

Manny was almost afraid to ask. "You took careful notes, I assume?"

"Of course. I'm not a complete idiot," Chris answered, working his way out of the suit.

"I've always told anyone who would listen that you're a partial idiot, with traces of genius."

"Thanks." Chris pushed his pant legs back down where they belonged.

"Well, on behalf of the department, thanks for your help. The system's up and running."

Chris tried to smooth some of the wrinkles out of his shirt. "What do you use it for, anyway? I saw some custom stuff in there, and one or two things that require government approval."

"I can't tell you."

"I'm eighty percent sure I saw a molecular sequencer in line with the logic pathway," Chris prodded, unwilling to give up so easily.

"I'm sorry. You know I can't tell you."

"Great. So all I get out of this is a hearty handshake?"

Manny smiled. "And the knowledge that you've helped a friend in need."

"That and twenty-five MUs will get me a bad cup of coffee."

Manny waited until Chris had stowed the body suit in a locker, and then the two of them headed across campus toward the Student Union Building, or SUB as the students called it. This was one of the few truly social spots at the academy. The Space Sciences Academy was built on Io, one of Jupiter's moons. A location close to Jupiter had been selected because the planet offered so many different opportunities for study and its moons presented an impressive array of geological diversity.

Chris and Manny were both in their third year at the academy and loved it. At seventeen, Chris was a year younger than his friend, but there were quite a few students on campus who had finished high school early in accelerated programs, so he was by no means the youngest student on campus.

They walked into the SUB and found an unoccupied table in

the lounge. After ordering drinks, Manny leaned forward and folded his hands on the table.

"Actually, I do have one other thing for you. I heard there's a shipment coming in tomorrow afternoon."

"So?"

"The freighter takes off in three days. You'll never guess the final destination."

"Perimeter One Station?"

Manny nodded, grinning. Chris let out a whoop and slammed his palm down on the table. A few people turned to look, but for the moment, Chris didn't care.

"Manfred, if you weren't my roommate, I'd kiss you."

"Then I'm glad I'm your roommate."

"Look out!"

The freighter lurched violently from side to side as the thin, weasel-faced man at the controls tried to charter a path through an asteroid field. The ship was fast but poorly shielded, and all three crew members knew a direct hit would be lethal.

"I can do it! Back off!"

The owner of the freighter, one Jerry Wysoski, lunged for the controls as chunks of rock flashed past the cockpit window, much too close for comfort. The largest of the crew members dragged the thin man out of the command chair and threw him against the wall.

"You idiot! Are you trying to get us killed?"

"I told ya, I've done it before," the weasel, also known as Sten, whined.

"Yeah? Well, I couldn't tell from looking."

Jerry settled into the command seat and throttled back, applying reverse thrust to slow the freighter down but never taking his eyes off the asteroids ahead. Actually, cutting through the asteroid belt had been his idea, and now he was seriously regretting it. They were hoping to gain some time, time they had lost at the last stop.

Their last stop had actually been another ship. The transstellar cruise liner *Gallant* was ten weeks into a trip from beyond the edge of the solar system and short on supplies. And this was no simple request for provisions, as the procurement officer had transmitted a list sporting such essentials as caviar, wine, and fortune cookies. The liner carried more than two thousand passengers and was nearly a quarter mile in length. The sheer size of the ship provided ample storage space, but every contingency could not be anticipated and sometimes there were shortfalls

As luck would have it, Jerry had received the transmission while refueling on the moon, and he was able to pick up all the items on the list. The problem had started shortly after the freighter docked with the cruise liner, out in the middle of nowhere. Jerry was busy negotiating his fee when he got an emergency call on his communicator. Apparently, while he was hard at work, one of his shipmates—a burly, unshaven man named Griff—had picked a fight with one of the passengers. The resulting disturbance was not appreciated by the ship's captain. Some fast talking and a substantially reduced fee were the only things that kept them out of the brig.

That had been three days ago, and not another word was said about the incident. But now as Jerry tried to navigate the asteroid field, he couldn't help thinking about it. A crippling impact from one of these disenfranchised rocks would be a perfect finish to a rotten trip.

"Will it really make that much of a difference if we're half a day late?" Sten asked.

Jerry tried to answer and still give the asteroids his full attention. "We're . . . taking perishable . . . medical supplies to . . . the Space Sciences Academy on Io. You think they're going to . . . pay us if the cargo is spoiled?"

Griff gazed steadily out the front window. "As captain of this ship, it's your responsibility to see to it we make enough of a profit to make the trip worth doing."

Jerry chewed on his lip to keep from swearing. A large rock flew past the port window, reminding him of the business at hand. "As crew members, it's . . . your responsibility to . . . use your heads once in a while, so I don't have to . . . use our fee to keep your sorry backsides out of jail."

It was on trips like these that Jerry really wished he could find a different crew. Jumping from one job to another without a break made it difficult to make personnel changes.

Griff continued with a definite edge in his voice. "If you keep blowing our fee, we have no alternative but to try and make a little extra on the side. There's always the chance a deal can go sour."

"I don't care what you do on your own time, so long as you stay out of trouble."

Griff bit down hard on his cigar. "Yes, sir."

The tension in the air was very thick, and one thing Jerry had learned over the years was how to change the subject. The freighter hit an open patch and he was able to ask Sten a question. "Tell me again, what are we picking up on Io?"

"I don't remember for sure. Your usual academy brat kind of stuff. Books, furniture, mail, who knows?"

"Who cares?" Griff growled around the butt of his cigar.

Sten ignored his shipmate, hoping he would cool down. "Oh, yeah. There was one interesting item. Several hundred pounds of trimagnasite on a return order."

Jerry frowned. "Someone must have misplaced a decimal point somewhere."

"It would be just like an academy brat to order something like that and change his mind."

"I'll carry anything they want. Just so long as it isn't something that spoils."

Sten forced a laugh and hazarded a glance at Griff. The look on the big man's face was not pleasant. Sten had seen that look before. If Griff didn't let off some steam before long, someone was going to die.

* * *

The aircab swung down out of the afternoon sky in a long, low arc, touching down on the expressway that fed into the Dulles Spaceport. Wheels down and wings retracted, the cab looked like any other ground car. Huddled in the backseat, the Grahams were hoping they weren't too late. Nathan looked nervously at his chronometer.

"We have ten minutes."

Ryan elbowed his sister in the ribs. "Nice work, Sis."

Nathan growled a warning. "Ryan."

Amie's cheeks were red. "It's not my fault! Mom, tell him it's not my fault."

Millie looked apologetically at her daughter. "We did have to repack your bag."

Ryan sneered at his sister. "Told you."

"All right. So there's not going to be any snow on a space station. Just rub it in, why don't you!"

The cab pulled up to the front of the terminal, and the Grahams grabbed their luggage and dashed inside. As their cab pulled away, another drove up, depositing a woman wearing a dark gray work suit. The woman looked to be in her late twenties and had a small duffel bag slung over her shoulder. She spotted the Grahams through the window and hurried inside.

The Grahams checked in, ran to their gate, down a flight of stairs, and hopped onto a bus, just as the doors were closing. Bags were stuffed into the luggage rack along the wall, and then they plopped into the nearest seat, letting out a collective sigh of relief.

The doors opened one last time, and the woman in the work suit stepped on. She walked immediately to the back, studiously ignoring the other passengers. The bus pulled away from the terminal, heading out across the concrete landscape. Looming in the distance was their ship.

"Whoa! Look at the size of that thing!" Ryan exclaimed.

The airship stood nearly forty feet high, not counting the space shuttle mounted on its back, and was as long as a football field. The heat shields on the aft hull would prevent damage from the shuttle's thrusters during blastoff.

The Grahams and a handful of other passengers stepped off the bus into an enclosed elevator, which rose slowly to shuttle level. A docking sleeve extended from the elevator, providing a covered walkway to the main entrance.

They found their assigned seats without trouble and stowed their bags. Ryan and Amie had window seats, with Millie and Nathan on the aisle. As the parents rummaged with seatbelts, the younger Grahams kept their eyes glued to the windows. Even Nathan, who had taken these trips a number of times, thought the view was impressive.

Ryan looked down as the airship started to taxi. "Hard to believe this thing will get off the ground."

Nathan smiled a little. "Wait till we really get rolling. You still won't believe it."

After several minutes, the airship lumbered into position at the end of a long runway, and the captain's voice came over the speakers.

"This is Captain Newman. Welcome aboard flight 2825 to McKinley Station. Transit time today will be forty-six minutes. As this is an orbital flight, we will not be providing a food or beverage service. Tucked in your seat pocket in front of you there should be a minisnack, which includes a juice packet. If there is any way we can make your trip more enjoyable, please don't hesitate to call the attendant."

Without delay, the airship started slowly down the runway, gradually picking up speed. They passed the liftoff speed for a normal transport, and still the wheels were solidly on the ground. After what seemed like forever, Ryan turned to his dad with a worried look on his face.

"We're still not off the ground. We're not going to run out of runway, are we?"

"He's got five miles to work with. We should be off the ground in another minute or so."

Sure enough, almost a minute later the wheels lifted off the ground, and the airship glided ponderously up into the late afternoon sky. Unlike ground to ground trips, the ship had no cruising altitude, so it kept climbing, leaving far below the ground and then the clouds, until the passengers could actually begin to see the curved horizon of the planet.

At Nathan's suggestion, the Grahams broke out the mini-snacks and started into the little sandwich wrapped inside. He handed out motion sickness pills to Millie and the children, and took one himself, to help them make the transition to weightlessness. At 60,000 feet, the shuttle engines fired and the shuttle separated from the airship, which immediately began its descent back to Earth.

The shuttle continued to climb until it was out of the Earth's atmosphere and travelling in orbit. The view was astonishing. Looking down, Ryan could see the continent of North America, both oceans, and even the edge of Europe. He had traveled away from Earth before, but the wonders of the voyage always amazed him.

It seemed like only moments later when the engines stopped firing, and the shuttle maneuvered into an orbit synchronous with McKinley Launching Station. A few more bursts from the engines, and they were on final approach. By pressing his face against the window, Ryan was able to see the launching station. Eight pods stuck out on eight spiral arms, octopus-like, from a central debarkation structure. The concept was simple: passengers disembarked from the shuttle at the central structure, walked to one of the spiral arms, and rode a conveyor belt out to the designated launch bay. Passengers arriving from other planets could hitch a ride on the next shuttle making a return trip to Earth. Shuttles came and went every ten minutes, so the wait was never long.

Ryan watched, fascinated, as the shuttle glided in and docked with the central structure by using positional thrusters to line up with the docking arms. An accordian-like passageway extended and sealed to the side of the shuttle as the seatbelt light overhead went out, and the captain's voice came over the speaker once more.

"Welcome to McKinley Station. The station does not rotate, so you will be weightless at all times. Any passenger needing orientation will find a hospitality suite inside the debarkation structure. Thank you for flying with us, and have a nice day."

The Grahams took a moment to fasten shoulder straps to some of their bags before slinging them over their arms, and then began pulling themselves along the aisle toward the front of the shuttle. The shuttle entrance, looking through the tube into the station, reminded Nathan of a football stadium back home. A tow rope mounted on one side of the tube made the rest of the journey easy; all they had to do was grab a handle and the rope did the rest.

McKinley Station was designed for one purpose—the orbital launching of space vessels—and had been built in the most utilitarian manner possible. While there were lounges and chairs bolted along the corridors, and even an occasional eatery, everything else about the place looked like it belonged in a sports arena. No decorations adorned the walls, and the structural supports were visible throughout. The predominant color was drab, gunmetal gray, but since nearly everyone on the station was only passing through, nobody seemed to care much about the surroundings.

As the Grahams entered the station, they were given shoe coverings by an attendant. The coverings were treated with a special substance which caused them to adhere to the metal decks of the station. They would be able to walk so long as one foot was on the deck at all times. It was not unusual to see a person who had tried to walk too fast floating free.

"I wouldn't want to live here," Millie observed, as they worked their way along the outer corridor which circled the debarkation structure.

"Actually, there are a few convenience quarters for the occasional traveler who gets stuck here between flights, but I wouldn't recommend them," Nathan replied.

Ryan thought this would be a great place for some serious exploring. "Do we have time before the flight to look around a little?"

Nathan shook his head. "Sorry, but I think we better head for the passenger liner to check in."

Absorbed in their conversation, the Grahams never noticed the woman in the work suit, who peered over her book from an upholstered chair nearby. As they passed out of earshot the woman spoke into a communicator.

"They're on their way."

The only light in the dark passageway was the small glow of a communicator held by a man pressed against the wall. After a moment, a voice came over the communicator.

"Excellent. I have been reviewing your plans. I am concerned about being implicated, or indirectly blamed for your . . . handiwork."

The figure in the dark was thoughtful for a moment. He had seen good plans unravel at this point in the process. The next few moments would be critical.

"How can you be blamed for a tragic accident? You want Graham and his work destroyed, don't you?"

"Yes."

"Then don't worry. You will be able to deny you knew anything. I guarantee you won't even know how it was done."

"Very well. Keep me informed of your progress, to the extent you can do so without compromising my position."

The man slipped the communicator into a jacket pocket and smiled at the darkness. So far, the plan was going perfectly.

Chris sat perfectly still in front of the desk in his dorm room. A small control panel was placed at an odd angle on the desk, surrounded by an assortment of cables, tools, and connectors. The quiet was shattered a moment later when Manny burst through the door.

"Sorry I'm late. I had a little trouble convincing the freighter pilot you were worthy cargo." Manny threw his coat in a corner and sat down on his bed.

"So I don't even qualify as freight? That hurts."

"Don't take it personally. These guys take packages mostly. There's more paperwork with actual passengers."

Chris stood up and stretched his legs. "Well, thanks for doing it, anyway."

"It was the least I could do after the way we treated MRV. How's the new one coming?"

"Done, I think. I still haven't tested it." Chris yawned and looked out the window.

Someone in the administration building had programmed an overcast sky for the mimetic display on the dome over the academy.

"What are you staring at?" Manny asked.

"The sky. It looks as drab as I feel."

"I hate to add to your problems, but midterms start tomorrow."

Chris winced. "I knew that. Thanks for reminding me."

"Sorry. I know you've missed a few classes this week. I figured you'd rather hear it now than tomorrow morning."

Chris checked the time. "They're not serving dinner anymore, are they?"

"No."

"I'll grab something at the SUB, then meet you at the library. We can hit the books until it closes."

In the dark silence of space, the passenger liner approached the space station. Just over one mile in diameter, the tremendous silver ring of the station spun slowly clockwise on its axis. This provided the illusion of gravity for those inside but created a rather dizzying display for the passsengers on the liner.

At 450 feet long, the liner contained about a hundred individual cabins, small but livable, all adjoining a long central common area. Intermittently along the walls were self-service food dispensers, individual video booths, and exercise equipment. Large windows in several lounges offered stunning views of the stars. Toward the front of the common area were three small shops, where passengers could purchase things necessary and not-so-necessary. The accommodations were nice enough, but a three-week trip from Earth still seemed very long squeezed into a ship with almost two hundred other people.

The liner slowed to a crawl, and four wide docking arms rotated out, locking into place. The resulting noise startled some of the less seasoned passengers, even as the ship continued its leisurely pace toward the station. On the starboard side of the liner, about fifty feet from the aft section, a bespectacled face with a tidy black mustache peered out one of the oval windows.

Nathan leaned back in his seat to give his son and daughter a better view.

"This is great!" Ryan said, brushing a lock of dark brown hair out of his eyes. "You can see the whole station from here!"

As the passenger liner came within a few hundred feet of the docking structure, the pilot deftly manipulated the controls until his ship was alongside the station, rotating at the same speed. After a few minutes of delicate adjustments, the docking arms of the ship made contact with the couplings on the station and then locked in. The Grahams collected their things and moved out of their cabin.

"Hey, they blacked the windows!" Ryan said, surprised.

"They activate the shades so that the swirling of the stars won't make anyone seasick," Nathan responded.

"*Space*-sick," Amie chimed in.

Her father smiled. "*Danke, Liebchen.*"

"*Bitte,*" she said, smiling back.

By this point, the crowd at the hatchway had dwindled to a few stragglers and crew members. The slow rotation of the ship meant that the passengers had to mind their balance, as the mild centrifugal force was pushing them away from the middle of the ship, toward the front and back. The Grahams leaned forward slightly to compensate, and then moved through the hatchway at an easy pace and on into the docking tunnel beyond. In a few short steps they were out in the unloading area.

This section appeared to fill most of the interior of the docking structure. Designed specifically for people arriving from long sojourns in cramped quarters, the wall across from the tunnel was imprinted with a three-dimensional image of lush green fields stretching off to majestic peaks in the distance. A cool fresh breeze wafted across the new arrivals, smelling delightfully of wild flowers and wet grass.

Following the image to the edge, Ryan noticed that the passengers ahead seemed to be streaming up the curved side walls of the room. A half dozen information booths were spaced evenly up the side walls, and there was one directly overhead. The view was dizzying, but the design made perfect sense. The illusion of gravity, mild though it was, required people to stand with their heads toward the center of the station as it rotated.

Looking up, Amie couldn't escape the feeling that people were walking on the ceiling, and it made her knees weak. Her mother put a steadying hand on her shoulder.

Nathan spoke, seeming to read everyone's thoughts. "It's going to take some getting used to. Until you feel more comfortable, just deal with your immediate surroundings."

"It's so . . . so . . . ," Millie gasped between breaths. The smells were so real, she could almost feel the cool grass between her toes.

"Breathtaking?" Nathan asked.

Millie only nodded. Nearly overcome by an impulse to run through the field in the picture, Amie scampered down the ramp with Ryan close behind. They sprinted to within a few feet of the wall and stopped suddenly. Up close, the vista became lost in the texture of the wall. Amie reached out and touched the rough surface.

"Why do so many things look better from a distance?" she sighed.

"Because your eyes aren't what they used to be!" Ryan called over his shoulder as he ran back to the ramp.

"That was a rhetorical question, you slug!" Amie hollered, charging after him.

"All right, you two," Nathan said reluctantly, not really wanting to spoil their fun. "That's enough dashing about."

Dotted here and there along the curved "floor" were protesters holding signs. The messages on the signs decried the immorality of colonization, but the protesters themselves seemed almost disinterested in their cause, as if they'd been at it too long.

"Dad, why are those people holding signs?" Ryan asked.

"They are part of a group who don't think we should colonize other planets. They call themselves 'Friends of the Galaxy' or FOG. We have to deal with them quite a lot at work."

"What have they got against SAFCOM?"

Nathan smoothed his mustache for a moment. "Since we're mostly a communications company, they think we're making it easier for humankind to expand. They've had people on the station for almost twenty years protesting the accelerator."

Amie eyed them suspiciously. "Are they dangerous?"

"They have a few nut cases in their ranks, but they're mostly harmless. The only one on our most wanted list is a nasty fellow named Ares Bouman."

Ryan's eyes brightened. "That guy who blows up stuff?"

21

"That's right. We haven't heard from him in a year or so."

Millie was puzzled. "What about the Milwaukee station three months ago?"

"That wasn't Bouman. Whenever he blows up one of our installations, he sends me a sympathy card."

"Well, at least he has a sense of humor," Amie said.

"Yes. A very dangerous one."

The docking bay was nearly empty by now and Nathan picked up his bags. "Everyone come with me, please. And stay close."

As a group they clumped down the ramp and along the floor to an information booth on the left side of the room, near a square platform set into the floor. Nathan waited patiently for the person in front of him to get directions and then stepped up to the counter. The traveler stepped to the side onto the square, and after a moment, the square dropped slowly through the floor, like an elevator on an aircraft carrier, and the person disappeared from view.

"Welcome to Perimeter One Station," the attendant said brightly. "How may I help you?"

"We're staying in quadrant four, deck C," said Nathan.

"And your room number?" she asked, turning her attention to her computer screen.

"Thirty-one," Nathan answered.

After a few moments, she looked up from her screen and said, "Dr. Nathan Graham?"

"That's me," he replied.

"It's an honor to have you here, sir. I have your party of four reserved for six days and five nights, with one more arrival tomorrow afternoon," she said, checking the screen.

"That's my oldest boy. His last final was five days ago. He's hitching a ride on a freighter."

"His ship will be landing in one of the landing bays—number five—at the outer edge of the station. Rooms on C deck in quadrant four are numbered one through forty. Stand on the square, please. When you reach the next level, turn right, go about one hundred feet and wait by the blue doors for the transporter to quadrant four. It should be along in a few minutes."

Nathan thanked the attendant and the Grahams gathered on the square next to the booth. The elevator dropped and they sank through the hole in the floor. Then they found themselves in a long, gray corridor, which curved up and away in both directions, like some crazy hallway around a giant stadium.

Nathan led them to the right, and they followed the hallway upward. But with each step, their location became the bottom again, as if the station were rotating under their feet at the exact pace they were walking. This was another illusion caused by the centrifugal force pressing them outward toward the edges of the station. On Earth, down was always down, but here "down" was "out" from wherever you happened to be at the moment.

The Grahams continued on until they came to a set of large, round, blue doors, with a white "4" in the center. The only peculiar thing was that the doors seemed to be set into the floor. The impression that with the doors open one would suddenly be standing at the edge of a deep shaft made everyone slightly nervous. In normal gravity, they would have put their bags down while they waited, but here that wasn't necessary.

"Is this where we get our gravity adjusted?" Ryan asked.

Nathan chuckled. "Sort of. As we move out—or down— toward the edge of the station, we will start to feel heavier because it's spinning. Because we've been weightless for three weeks, we have to take it pretty slow. The trip to C deck is about a half mile, but it will probably take two and a half hours." Ryan and Amie groaned, while Millie eyed their current drab surroundings.

"I liked the unloading area better," she said a little wistfully.

Less than a minute later, the doors hissed open, and a small lounge rose up out of the floor. The transporter was round and reminiscent of the inside of a shuttle bus, containing a number of electronic games and library devices and furnished with padded sofas to help pass the time in relative comfort. Amie and Ryan sat down at the games console, while Millie slipped off her shoes and lay down on a sofa. Nathan had found from painful experience that his joints made the transition to gravity much better if he stayed on his feet.

The doors closed overhead, and the transporter started its slow trek from the docking structure through space toward the outer edges of the ring. Over the next half hour, the view nearly took their breath away. The vista of the surrounding station was astonishing. With each passing minute, they could see more and more of the docking structure with the passenger liner still attached, all against a vivid backdrop of stars.

Despite misgivings on Amie's part, Ryan convinced her to join him in a chess game. Though he was a gifted player and had won several tournaments, she refused to accept any handicap. The first game was over in nine moves, the second in fifteen, while the third actually went on for some time.

As Millie watched her children play, she was impressed that Amie didn't get upset as she was demolished time after time. Ryan seemed to be as gracious a winner. Several times he gently tried to help and encourage his sister. Those were the moments that always warmed her heart.

Ryan looked up from the games console. "Dad, did you ever meet Ares Bouman?"

"He used to come and see me almost every week."

"You met with a terrorist every week?" Ryan asked, wide-eyed.

Nathan smiled a little and sighed, looking out the window and remembering. "He wasn't a terrorist then. Just a passionate activist in a relatively harmless organization, trying to change interstellar laws and public opinion to his way of thinking."

"What happened to him?"

"No one knows exactly. He was living in Washington, D.C., at the time. Rushing across town from a Senate subcommittee meeting to a fund-raiser, he was involved in a ground car accident. He lost his wife in the crash, and some say he just snapped. Others think he just got tired of trying to work within the law and took matters into his own hands."

Ryan was really interested. "What do you think?"

"I think it was probably a little of both. Whatever the reason, he is now very dangerous and should be put away."

"He blows up *things,* right? Not people."

"He started out that way, but it was only a matter of time before somebody got killed. Once that happens, you have to decide whether you're willing to kill for your cause. Bouman decided he was willing. After a few accidental deaths, it didn't seem to matter to him anymore." Nathan dismissed the unpleasant memories with a wave of his hand. "What's done is done."

Ryan caught the hint and went back to the game console with Amie. Millie took in the view for as long as her eyes would stay open, and then she fell asleep. The next thing she knew, it was two hours later and the transporter was dropping through another set of double doors, depositing them on C deck. The transporter seemed to end in the middle of the section where the passenger quarters were. Here, the lighting was bright and the decorations more suitable for a resort hotel than a space station.

Heartened, but now feeling the full weight of gravity, they trudged down the hallway in search of room 31, looking more like prisoners on a death march than honored guests. As they reached the door to their room, Nathan noticed his wife nearly collapsing under the weight of her luggage. Responding to the question on his face, she said simply, "I need to be more careful what I buy in zero gravity."

Nathan inserted his card key into the lock, and the entire family tumbled through the door, dropping their baggage unceremoniously on the floor. Without a word, each one picked a bed and promptly fell into it.

"Good idea," Nathan said thickly, "we'll take a quick nap

and worry about unpacking. . . ." His voice trailed off. At this particular moment, he didn't care if they ever unpacked.

Nathan awoke with a start sometime later. He had been dreaming—about a heart attack. He tried to sit up and found that the crushing weight on his chest had not departed with the dream. Even as panic rose in his throat, he remembered where he was and stifled a chuckle of relief, amused by his own foolishness. After a few deep breaths, he rolled over and pushed himself up to a sitting position. "Not too bad," he thought, and decided to try standing. His leg muscles complained a little bit, but movement was getting easier with each passing moment.

Moving to a nearby table, he turned on the small lamp and found the folder of guest services. There was a map of the entire station, with their room marked in red, folded in the inside front pocket. With his finger, he began tracing paths from their door to the various services that were available. Restaurants, shops, and swimming pools abounded, along with two arboretums, four movie theaters, and a low-gravity gymnasium.

The map looked odd at first, because the cross section of the station showed facilities mounted on the walls of each segment. Nathan had to stop thinking of it as a "top view" and remind himself that as the station rotated, "down" was outward from the center, and the walls in the map were actually floors.

The space station's internal layout was much like a long, forty-story hotel, rolled up along its length until the ends joined. Though a mile across, the disk was only six hundred feet wide from side to side. The interior design was open and bright, however, which kept most people from feeling hemmed in. There were passages, stairways, and transport tubes to get from place to place. Unless you stayed on one deck and walked the entire circumference, the station didn't seem nearly as confining as it looked on paper.

Nathan looked up from the map to see his wife gingerly climbing out of her bed. She had that wonderful, sleepy-faced, tousled look she always had right after waking up. She shuffled across the floor, feeling a little wobbly, to look at the map.

"I thought I was having a heart attack," she said, a little ruefully.

"Me, too," he replied, brushing a strand of hair out of her eyes and kissing her on the cheek.

She pointed to the room marked in red.

"This is us?" she asked.

"Yes," he replied, preparing to take her on his recently completed finger tour of the facilities. Yawning, she nodded and looked away, unable to cope with the map for the moment. Turning from the table, she walked to the kitchen to find something to eat. She found a light switch and turned it on.

"Nice," she said to no one in particular.

Ryan stirred in his bed, and without opening his eyes, tried to sit up. "This is great, Dad," he said flatly, "how long am I going to feel like this?"

Nathan smiled apologetically. "It should only last a few minutes once you stand up."

Ryan lurched to his feet and winced. "Ow. Are we having fun yet?"

He stumbled over to the table and looked over his father's shoulder at the map. All at once, Amie rolled over and stood up.

"Oh, my," she said, weaving slightly.

"Take it slowly, dear," said her mother from the kitchen, "you'll feel better in a few minutes."

After puttering around the room for a half hour, they all began to notice how hungry they were. Having made themselves presentable, they headed out the door in search of a real meal.

At the end of the passenger quarters, the passage widened into a broad thoroughfare, with potted plants and all manner of people milling about. Lush green plants seemed to spring from nowhere, creating a very pleasant atmosphere in the corridor.

They walked a short distance and came to a cafe called simply *The Rosewood*, after the beautiful paneling and ornately carved furniture. Several tables sat outside for *al fresco* dining, even if there was no sky overhead. A young man seated them and the Grahams pored over the menu. It was difficult deciding what to order. When you've been eating spaceline food for three weeks, everything looks good.

Ryan looked up from his menu and did a double take. Across the restaurant stood a small, middle-aged man, wearing some sort of uniform. He was staring intently at them. Ryan stared back for a moment, then shrugged and returned to his menu. He couldn't shake the feeling of being watched, but when he looked up again, the man was gone. The only exit from the cafe appeared to be right past their table. His stomach growled, and he dismissed the mystery in favor of a quick decision about dinner.

The meal passed quickly, as conversation gave way to the more important business of eating. Once Nathan had given the waiter their room number for the bill, the family proceeded across the way to a cozy little lounge with thick, orange carpet and plush loveseats. They sat down to give their dinners a chance to settle.

"About tomorrow," Nathan began. "The symposium starts at nine. Millie, I thought you might want to make arrangements for a tour of the accelerator the day after tomorrow."

"Good idea," Millie replied. "Where do you make reservations?"

Nathan's eyebrows went up. "I don't know. I guess we'll have to find it on the map. When is Chris supposed to get here?"

Millie reached into her handbag and pulled out a slip of paper. "He's due to arrive about four-thirty tomorrow afternoon. He left Jupiter three days ago."

"Only a four-day trip? I keep forgetting what time of year it is," Nathan said, pulling a card out of his shirt pocket. He studied it for a moment. "We're actually quite close to Jupiter now. The trip won't be pleasant, but it will be mercifully short.

"At any rate, Ryan and Amie will have most of the day to get acquainted with their new surroundings."

Ryan looked around the lounge. "Do they have any . . . ?" His voice trailed off. From the far side of the lounge, the little man from the cafe sat staring right at him.

"Do they have any what?" asked Nathan.

Ryan turned to his father and said in a hushed whisper, "Dad, do you see that guy over there?"

"What guy?"

The man was gone again. Ryan practically ran to the other side of the lounge, but there was no sign of the mystery man. Again, the only apparent exit was right past where they were sitting. Ryan walked back, bewildered, and flopped in his seat.

"I must be seeing things," he said at last.

"Tell me what you saw, Ryan," his father said gently.

"Well, first there was this guy in the restaurant staring at us. I didn't think much about it at first, but then it started to bug me. So I decided to look him over, but then he was gone. Then we came in here and sat down, and I noticed him sitting across the room staring at us. And now he's gone again."

Nathan frowned slightly. "What did he look like?" As a forensic scientist, he had spent long hours in public places with his children playing games of observation. The pastime had paid dividends more than once.

Ryan closed his eyes and tried to picture the man. "Forty-ish, dark hair with a little gray, light build with a blue and gray uniform. No visible distinguishing marks." He opened his eyes and his father smiled proudly.

"Very good. And you're not seeing things. The uniform you described is standard issue to station personnel."

"Well, that's a relief."

"Maybe you should give my speech tomorrow." Nathan stretched his arms. "How about we look around a little bit and then call it a night. We have a busy day tomorrow."

There was agreement all around and the Grahams wandered out into the passageway to see what other amenities C deck had to offer. Along the walls were dozens of businesses, including a grocery store, gift shops, hair salons, video arcades, law offices, even a music store. Nathan was glad his family tried never to buy anything on credit. Every product in the stores was marked up 300 percent over the most expensive tourist traps he had seen on Earth.

It was several hours later that they returned to their room worn out, but excited. They took some time to unpack before finalizing sleeping arrangements.

"This place is even better than you said." Ryan yawned, sitting down to take his shoes off.

"I didn't want to get your hopes up before you'd seen it," his father replied. "I haven't been out here for quite a while. I wasn't sure it would be as nice as I remembered."

Amie stepped into the bathroom and turned on the light. "It's going to be nice to take a normal shower," she said, closing the door and locking it.

Mrs. Graham sat down to remove her shoes and glanced at the table. "Nathan!" she cried, her voice edged with fear. Nathan turned sharply and was by her side in an instant. Millie was pointing to the table. Scrawled on their map in large, red letters was the message: YOU ARE IN GREAT DANGER. PLEASE LEAVE AT ONCE.

Nathan picked up the map angrily and wadded it up, tossing it on the kitchen counter.

Millie was frightened. "What does it mean?"

"It means we'll have to get a new map."

His wife looked up from the table and saw his look of concern. "Should we report it?" she asked.

"Not until we know who our friends are," Nathan replied.

"What is it, Dad?" Ryan asked from his bed.

Nathan picked up the crumpled map and threw it to his son. "Just a message from someone who is concerned for our safety."

Ryan opened the map, read the message and said, "Cool. This place just gets better and better."

Nathan took the map back, crumpled it up again, and then

threw it in the disposal. "Don't tell your sister about this. I don't want to scare her."

"Not a word," said Ryan, pretending to zip his lips.

Millie proceeded to remove her shoes, trying to put the message out of her mind. She was not a great fan of adventure. A few minutes later Amie walked out of the bathroom and walked over to her mother.

"Can I borrow your hairbrush?" she asked sleepily. Millie opened her handbag and began fishing around inside.

"Hey, where's the map?" Amie asked, noticing its absence.

"Your father threw it away," her mother replied, not looking up.

"Why?"

Her mother handed her the hairbrush. "Because he felt like it."

"But it was a perfectly good map. Why would he throw it away?"

Millie glared at her husband. "Your children are too blasted observant. She's your daughter. You tell her."

Nathan motioned for his daughter to sit down and then joined her across the table. He hoped she would take the news all right. He had learned the hard way that twelve-year-olds are unpredictable.

"While you were in the bathroom, your mother discovered a message written on the map."

"What did it say?"

"That we were in danger and should leave right away."

Amie pondered that for a moment. "Are we leaving?" she said at last.

"No," her father said. "Not yet, anyway."

"Good," she said, obviously relieved. "I'd hate to have one stupid note spoil our fun."

Millie smiled at that, and Nathan patted his daughter on the shoulder. "Well said, *Liebchen*. Let's get some rest."

The Grahams got ready for bed and turned in for the night, unaware that they were being watched.

CHAPTER 2

While the rest of his family drifted off to sleep, Chris Graham was many thousands of miles away in the cargo hold of a small freighter. Squeezed between two large, plastic boxes with his duffel bag and backpack, he was trying unsuccessfully to get some sleep. He rolled over for the third time in as many minutes and sat up.

"This is turning into a long trip," he said to his duffel bag.

He remembered the thrill of excitement he had felt when he heard there was a freighter headed this way, leaving on the day of his last final. He smiled mirthlessly. Still, it was better than not going at all, and you couldn't beat the price.

The trip had started out okay. He'd spent his first three hours on board pumping the command crew with questions about the engines until they threatened to shove him out the air lock. Freighter crews were a funny bunch, and altogether impossible to understand, so he'd decided the best course of action was to get out of their collective face.

He wasn't impressed with his living arrangements, but he'd seen the crew's quarters, and since they weren't much better than his, he didn't feel he had a right to complain. They did have furniture instead of boxes, however.

He looked around the cargo hold for the hundredth time and found absolutely nothing of interest. He considered breaking the seal on one of the boxes, but figured that would get him thrown off the ship for sure.

He opened his backpack and noticed his Bible, almost buried under the textbooks. He pulled it out, opened it up to the Gospel of John, and started reading about the life of Jesus.

He read for a while and gradually found himself caught up in the story. The events were all familiar, yet somehow different when considered in the unmitigated quiet of the cargo hold. When he closed his eyes, he could actually see the Nazarene carpenter turning water into wine at a wedding; fencing verbally with Pharisees in the synagogue; walking long dusty roads with his disciples; hanging in agony on a cross made of wood; standing in the garden outside his own empty tomb, very much alive. Chris closed his eyes and began to pray, but in exhaustion soon fell fast asleep.

He was awakened sometime later by a banging on the door. "Hey kid! You okay in there?" It was Jerry, one of the pilots.

Chris got up and opened the door. "Yeah, I'm fine. What's up?"

"Well, you didn't show up for dinner or breakfast and I wanted to be sure you were okay."

Chris looked in disbelief at his chronometer and found that it was halfway through the next day. Considering the generally anti-social attitude of most freighter pilots, he was surprised they had checked at all.

When Chris didn't speak, Jerry repeated, "You're sure you're all right?"

"Yeah. I feel great. When's lunch? I'm starving."

"About an hour and a half. I'll see you then." Jerry turned and started down the narrow hallway.

"Sounds good. Hey, Jerry. . . ." The pilot stopped and turned. "Thanks for checking."

The barest hint of a smile touched the corners of Jerry's mouth. "Sure," he said and was gone.

Chris went back inside the cargo hold and closed the door.

He couldn't remember the last time he had felt this rested. Maybe this wouldn't be such a long trip after all.

Morning came to the space station in its own unusual way. Since one flat side of the station was always facing the sun, the illusion of a diurnal cycle had been created artificially. Clocks on all the stations in the solar system were set to the same mean time to make life less traumatic for frequent travelers. On Perimeter One Station, at 6:00 A.M. SMT (Solar Mean Time), illumination in all unrestricted passageways increased slowly over a half hour's time to simulate dawn.

Auxiliary air vents created gentle breezes, and the temperature gradually increased from 65 to 72 degrees. This carefully orchestrated "daybreak" went largely unnoticed by guests of the station, but exit surveys had shown a noticeable psychological impact for those who had spent time on other stations. The surveys repeatedly contained statements about feeling "less cooped-up" and "more at home" than on any other station.

In the Grahams' room, Ryan bounded out of bed at 6:15 A.M. Nathan opened his eyes briefly and mused that there were definite benefits to being fifteen years old. Ryan reached down to pull a towel out of his bag, and Amie used that opportunity to scramble out of bed and make a mad dash for the bathroom. Her brother noticed too late and had made only a couple of steps when she slammed the door and locked it.

"Aw, Amie, you pig," Ryan groaned, forgetting his parents were in the room.

"Don't talk to your sister like that," Nathan mumbled into his pillow.

"But I was about to use the bathroom. She'll be in there for an hour."

"That's no excuse for calling your sister names." Nathan yawned. "Amie!"

"Yes?" The voice from the bathroom positively dripped with sweetness.

"Ten minutes and not a minute more," her father said, leaving no room for discussion.

"Of course, Daddy. We wouldn't want Ryan to miss his shower and stink up the whole station."

Ryan bit his tongue, threw down his towel, and flopped on the bed, trying to think of something nasty he could do to his sister without getting caught.

Mrs. Graham rolled over onto her back, but refused to open her eyes. "Why don't these things have master bedrooms?" she huffed, sleepily.

Her husband turned in her general direction without opening his eyes. "There's a limited amount of space. I'm sure they had to forgo some luxuries during design."

"Soundproof master bedrooms," she said, pretending not to hear him.

Forty-five minutes later, all four of them were showered, dressed, and sitting informally around the kitchen table.

"Before we go and grab some breakfast," Nathan announced, "I thought we should talk about our plans for the day."

"I want to go exploring!" Ryan said excitedly.

"Me too!" Amie chimed in.

"Fine," said Nathan, "just be sure you stick together."

Ryan looked sick at the thought of having his little sister tag along, but nodded glumly, knowing this was not negotiable. Mrs. Graham reached into her handbag and pulled out a list, explaining that she wanted to shop for groceries before the symposium started and make arrangements for the tour of the accelerator. With that settled, they headed out in search of breakfast.

This time, they walked past *The Rosewood* and found a festive little omelette parlor with stucco walls and a southwestern motif. Walking on the station used much more energy than when they had been on the ship, and the extra effort was making them ravenous. Fortunately, the omelette parlor specialized in generous portions.

When they had finished eating, the Grahams located an information booth and picked up additional station maps. The family found a private spot in a nearby lounge and joined hands. Nathan led them in a prayer for the day, and when they were finished, they moved back out into the corridor.

Millie gave Amie a quick hug, while Nathan patted Ryan on the shoulder. "Have fun, you two. Try to stay out of trouble."

Nathan mussed Ryan's hair, and the family went their separate ways.

Ryan and Amie quickly found a stairway and ran outward, or downward as they saw it, to B deck, which was much like C deck in layout. Only here they felt heavier, and there were different shops to explore. Ryan pulled out his map and studied it for a moment.

"Hey, there's a movie theater in the next quadrant. Let's check it out."

Amie noticed that some of the shops were just opening up. "I want to look in some of these stores first."

"Aw, Amie, come on." Shopping was not his idea of a good time.

"We have all day," she replied, turning into a souvenir shop.

Ryan stood still a moment, contemplating ditching his sister, but he knew he'd be in serious trouble if his dad found out. With a sigh of resignation, he sauntered into the shop. All manner of plates, paper weights, and bric-a-brac stamped with the name of the station cluttered his vision. There were small working models of the station itself, coins, and other memorabilia littering low tables and Plexiglas shelves. Amie was standing off to the side holding a doll dressed in the official station personnel uniform.

"Aren't you a little old for dolls?" he said, needling her.

"I was just looking," she said, hastily putting the doll back.

Ryan was already bored. "Come on, Amie, let's go."

"Just a minute." She moved with infuriating slowness to the next table.

After what seemed like an eternity, she breezed past her brother and out the door with a perky "Come on." Ryan thought about giving her a good whack. Visions of his father giving *him* a good whack kept his hands firmly in his pockets, and he followed her without a word. They darted in and out of countless shops, and he began to have fun in spite of himself.

It was only after they had travelled some distance down the broad corridor of B deck, that Ryan stopped to see how far they had come. There, about fifty paces behind them, trying to look inconspicuous, was the little man from the cafe. Ryan turned the other way and quickened his pace slightly.

"Amie!" he said with hushed excitement. "Don't look now, but that guy from last night is following us!"

She sneaked a hasty glance despite the admonition and quickened her pace to catch up with her brother.

"The little man in the uniform?" she asked.

"That's him."

"Doesn't look like much of a threat, even if he is following us."

"Yeah, but don't you want to know why?" Ryan said, sounding very much like his father.

"I suppose we'll find out eventually. Or he'll stop following us. Either way, the situation should resolve itself."

Ignoring his sister's ambivalence, Ryan decided to run a test. He grabbed his sister's arm and cut down a side passageway containing some self-service machines and a tiny hair salon. They ducked into the doorway of the salon and glanced back. The little man rounded the corner and pretended to use one of the machines.

"I knew it," Ryan said, rather pleased with himself.

"That doesn't prove anything. He's just using one of those machines."

"Yeah, but the one he's using is out of order."

He stepped out of the doorway and headed back to the main passage with Amie in tow. The man paid them no attention as they walked by, but as soon as they rounded the corner and headed down the corridor, he resumed his position fifty paces behind them.

Finally, Ryan couldn't stand it any longer. He pulled out his map and furrowed his brow, his eyes almost crossing with concentration. After a few moments, he stuffed the map into his pocket, grabbed Amie by the hand, said, "Come on!" and then took off at a dead run. Amie stumbled once, but caught her balance and quickly fell in step.

Quite a few people were roaming about by now, so they quickly found themselves dodging bodies, weaving frantically in and out of the crowd, until Ryan saw the stairway he was looking for. They dashed up the stairs two at a time and were back on C deck. They lurched across the passageway and hid behind a large bush, watching the top of the stairway. After a minute with no sign of the man, Ryan stood up.

"I think we lost him."

Amie was exasperated, "Why didn't you just walk up and ask him why he was following us?"

"That would have been too easy. Come on." He set off in search of the next quadrant. Amie followed reluctantly, thinking about giving *him* a good whack.

While Millie reserved seats for a tour of the accelerator, Nathan was busy in the conference hall renewing old acquaintances and friendships. The subject of the symposium was "Developments in Signal Acceleration and Their Relation to Temporal Phenomena." Many of the conference participants were people he had worked with at one time or another.

He scanned the room looking for familiar faces. Over next to the bar was the vice president of research and development from his company. SAFCOM was one of the first transsolar corporations to be established, with offices in the Terran solar system and the nearby Jemini solar system.

The Jemini system was smaller and partly manmade. When

manned space flight breached the perimeter of Earth's solar system, scientists were surprised to discover a large collapsed star only a few hundred million miles beyond. After decades of research into this cosmic wonder, a team of scientists hit upon a theoretical procedure for reversing the implosion of the collapsar.

After a 1.5-million-page Galactic Impact Statement, the team tested their theory and the result was a small star, which created three relatively hospitable planets. The life expectancy for the star was only five hundred thousand years, but colonies quickly sprang up in the resurrected solar system. The new system was christened "Gemini," though with only five satellites it was hardly a twin of the nine-satellite Terran solar system. After some debate and congressional legislation, the name was changed to "Jemini" to avoid confusion with the constellation.

When the need finally arose for the two systems to communicate, SAFCOM landed the contract. Dr. Graham was hired shortly thereafter along with hundreds of other engineers, to help design a tremendous signal accelerator at the edge of Earth's solar system. Upon completion of the project, he worked his way up the corporate ladder until, twenty-five years later, he was now head of the forensic sciences department for the entire company, which had grown to over two hundred thousand employees—the largest communications company in the solar system.

Nathan continued searching the room for familiar faces, and he broke into a broad grin as his eyes lit upon a round, almost cherubic-looking fellow. The man was none other than Dr. Jacob Barber, a close associate and dear friend with whom he had always intended to keep in close touch. Jacob Barber had been on the same accelerator design team as Dr. Graham.

He started toward his old friend but stopped suddenly, and his smile faded. It appeared that Dr. Barber was in the middle of a heated discussion with Dr. Andrews Mader. Mader had been hired the same time as Graham to help design the accelerator. . . .

Young Nathan Graham rode in a small, two-man shuttle from his cramped crew quarters toward the command staging area. The cluster of hundreds of environment modules—or "space trailers" as the workers called them—where the design and construction crews slept, were cabled together around the larger central planning structure that housed the managers and supervisors. The effect was comforting, like a small city floating in space.

Nathan had been on the design team for only three months, but already he was special assistant to his group leader, Dr. Joseph Misenberg. Construction was beginning on the first rings of the gargantuan signal accelerator and they were in danger of falling behind schedule.

A communication from Earth that had arrived for Nathan the day before revealed a fatal flaw in the designs for the accelerator. His good friend and team member Jacob Barber had counseled him not to make waves, but Nathan was notoriously bad about keeping his mouth shut when an important idea was hatching.

Nathan didn't mind working in space. But these short trips in tiny ships, with the infinite depth of the void all around and only the environment modules as a reference point, were enough to make anyone edgy. The atmosphere of the meeting he broke into was already tense.

Six people sat at the table, and two were standing near the door. At his entrance, several of the participants gave him exasperated looks. These were the managers for one of the biggest construction projects ever undertaken, and they had better things to do with their time. After an uncomfortable pause, one of the two who were standing took him by the arm and gently pulled him aside.

"This better be important, Nate," Dr. Misenberg said somberly.

Nathan swallowed hard and nodded, acutely aware that even though he held a Ph.D., he was seriously lacking in credibility with this particular group of high-powered engineers. Never mind that he graduated at the head of his class, with honors. These people knew he had little experience. He tried to keep his voice from shaking.

"I know this is irregular and I appreciate your willingness to rearrange your schedules to meet like this."

The president and general manager, Dr. Vorvick Shaw, was impatient. "Please get to the point, Dr. Graham."

"The point is, Dr. Shaw, we are going to have a power fall-off once we pass the four hundred mile point. With the current design, we can add boosters at regular intervals, but we will still suffer signal degradation after four hundred miles."

Dr. Shaw leaned back in his seat, trying to keep a condescending smirk off his face. "How is it, Dr. Graham, that a team of three hundred and fifty engineers missed such a critical flaw, and you had the remarkable brilliance to discover it all by yourself?"

A couple of the others smiled, and Nathan flushed, but an encouraging look from Dr. Misenberg gave him the strength to continue.

"Yesterday, I received a report from Earth." He held up a sheaf of papers. "These are the results of a two-year study by the metallurgy departments from MIT, Stanford, and the Space Sciences Academy on Io. According to this study, the alloy we are using to build the rings produces some unforeseen electromagnetic effects when current is passed through it over long distances. The net result is that toward the end of the accelerator, the rings themselves will bleed off enough power to drain signal integrity."

Dr. Shaw held out his hand and Nathan handed out copies of the report to the men and women sitting around the table. After several minutes of intense study, the prevailing silence told Nathan they knew he was right. Dr. Misenberg looked at Nathan, with a hint of a smile around his eyes.

"Thank you for bringing this to our attention, Dr. Graham. Do you have a proposed solution?"

"Actually I do, sir. If we gradually reduce the size of the rings as we go along, we can refocus the signals, and reduce the power fall-off to acceptable levels. I have some preliminary drawings here."

Dr. Shaw looked up sternly. "Please leave the drawings with us and return to your quarters."

Nathan nodded and caught Dr. Misenberg's wink as he turned to go. Relieved, he walked out of the room.

The designs for the first part of the accelerator did not have to be modified, so construction continued on schedule for several weeks. Nathan was given increasing authority by Dr. Misenberg, and he suddenly found himself working fifteen hours a day. He got into the habit of taking designs back to his quarters, which meant he had little time for socializing.

One evening, as he studied the plans for a hexagonal joint that connected the ring segments, he found another error. Baffled, he checked the numbers and then rechecked them, working backward until he found that the original error came from another design team's drawings. The next morning, he asked for another emergency meeting of the managing engineers.

Dr. Shaw was irritated. "What is it this time, Dr. Graham?"

Nathan felt more confident as he spread the drawing out on the table. "I found an error in the specs for the hex joint. The specs came from Murray Johnson's group."

Murray Johnson was brought in, and a rigorous check of his designs pointed to yet another team, Alpha Group, which reported to Dr. Shaw. Dr. Andrews Mader, the head of Alpha Group, was called in with his hex joint specs, and the managers gathered around to examine the drawings.

After several minutes, Dr. Misenberg pointed at a specific

spot on the drawing. "Here it is. In the fifth term of the calibration constant, the four and five are transposed."

He pulled out a calculator and did some quick, very complex calculations. "How many rings have we built so far?"

"Twelve," Dr. Shaw replied, looking darkly at Dr. Mader.

"They will have to be dismantled and the design drawings redone. The joints are too large for the gauge of the cables inside the rings."

Dr. Shaw glared at Nathan. "Once again, thank you for bringing this to our attention, Dr. Graham. You may leave now."

Andrews Mader gave Nathan such a murderous look that Nathan shuddered and hurried out of the room. He had found the error and was honor-bound to report it. But now he realized his actions had brought about the ruin of a man's career.

The redesign of the accelerator set the project back three months, and the prime contractor lost a large portion of the award fee for that period. Dr. Vorvick Shaw was demoted from his position as president and general manager to group leader, and Dr. Andrews Mader was summarily discharged.

Dr. Joseph Misenberg was promoted to Dr. Shaw's old position, and Nathan was made his vice president of operations, because of his early discovery of the flawed design and by special request of Dr. Misenberg. Despite the delays, the Misenberg Accelerator, as it was called at the dedication, was completed on schedule and under budget. Dr. Mader never spoke to Nathan again. . . .

Thoughts of the past swirled through Nathan's mind as he made his way across the room. With some trepidation he walked up beside Jacob Barber and Andrews Mader and waited to be noticed.

". . . I still say the power consumption curve is too steep. If you truncate the extensions using propylterethane materials . . ." Jacob's voice trailed off as he noticed the familiar figure standing patiently on his left.

"Nate!" he cried. The two men exchanged a bear hug and then stood at arm's length, looking each other over.

"The years have been kind to you," Jacob said at last, "but what's that thing on your lip?"

"It's called a mustache. I grew it about ten years ago. Millie liked it, so I kept it."

Both men became aware that they were excluding the third member of the conversation.

"Nathan Graham, I believe you know Dr. Andrews Mader."

"I do," said Nathan, cautiously extending his hand.

Dr. Mader quickly shook the proffered hand, gave Nathan a thin-lipped smile, and said without conviction, "It's good to see you again."

"Likewise," Nathan responded, trying to sound as if he meant it. He studied the man's face and saw that the years had not been kind to him. Hard lines of bitterness were etched around his mouth, and the smooth skin around his eyes bespoke a man who did not smile very often. There was a long moment of awkward silence, broken at last by Nathan.

"Well, I didn't mean to interrupt. . . ."

"I was just leaving." Dr. Mader turned and disappeared into the crowd.

"Andrews hasn't gotten any better with age, has he?" Nathan said, a little sadly.

"He goes by 'Dr. Mader' now, and no, he hasn't. What a waste."

Nathan shook his head. "Apparently he still blames me for his discharge."

"Everyone knows you were only doing your job. Besides, you didn't know it was his mistake when you reported it."

"But no one could ever convince him of that."

"No one could ever convince him of anything. You did your best."

"I just wish things had turned out differently, that's all."

Jacob grabbed his friend's hand and clapped it several times in an effort to break the mood. "Enough of this foolishness! Nathan, how have you been?"

Nathan mentally shook himself, and smiled at his friend. "Very well, Jacob, and yourself?"

"Never better. I had a heart attack five years ago and have been exercising ever since."

"Well, I'm glad God wasn't finished with you yet."

Jacob laughed at that. "Life is really much too interesting to hang it up just yet. How are Millie and those two adorable children?"

"Actually, it's three adorable children."

"It has been a while, hasn't it. How are they?"

"All doing very well. I brought them along."

"You did! We must have dinner together. So your oldest . . . um, Chris, isn't it? . . . he's here too?"

"He's due to arrive this afternoon. Coming in on a freighter from Io."

"I saw his name on the admissions roster for the academy. You must be very proud."

"Very." Nathan glanced around the room and then said apologetically, "Forgive me, but I have at least a dozen other people I should say hello to before we get going. Are you free for dinner tonight?"

"For you and your family, I am always free." Jacob's smile spread to the outer reaches of his round face.

Sometime later, Millie Graham wandered into the conference hall, just as people were beginning to take their seats. She edged her way around the room and found her husband already seated at one of the front tables. He checked his chronometer and smiled, knowing how much she disliked socializing with scientists.

"Jacob is here," he said, once she was settled.

"Jacob Barber?"

"Yes. He wants to have dinner with us."

"Oh, yes, let's. He is well?"

"He looks better than he ever has."

The master of ceremonies came to the podium and began introductions for the symposium. Almost immediately he was interrupted by a man at the back, yelling about inhumanity to the universe. In a matter of a few seconds two uniformed security guards hustled him out of the conference hall.

"Who was that?" Millie asked out loud.

"Probably one of those FOG nuts," Nathan replied, not trying to hide his disgust.

The emcee resumed his introductions. As Millie heard the topics that were going to be discussed, she found she was really looking forward to the morning presentations. She didn't get much time to brush up on the latest technology, so this was a real treat.

"I'm not going to any stupid control center."

"It's just two decks down and one quadrant over. Come on," Ryan said, studying his map.

"But. . . ." Amie sighed in frustration and ran after her brother.

At that moment, several hundred thousand miles away, Chris threw his head back and laughed. Jerry was not as amused, but a smile played at the corners of his mouth. The other two men at the table looked decidedly unfriendly.

"I can't believe you thought I was bluffing."

"Craziest bit of dumb luck I've ever seen," one of the men mumbled, chewing the cold, soggy butt of his cigar.

"It ain't right," the other replied, deadpan.

Jerry looked at the storm clouds brewing over his two associates and decided it was time to end the game. "Maybe we should call it quits."

Chris was oblivious. "You want to quit? No way. I'm on a roll."

Jerry chose his next words very carefully. "Would you like to continue the game outside?"

Chris suddenly caught on and looked sharply from Jerry to the two men. The smile left his face in a hurry.

"Suddenly, I'm incredibly thirsty," he said as nonchalantly as he could manage. He stood up, careful to leave his winnings behind. He walked casually over to the door. Jerry joined him a moment later. The two men were busy not noticing.

"Buy me a drink?" Jerry asked.

"Gladly," Chris replied, following him out into the narrow hallway.

Neither one of them said a word until they reached the galley. Jerry opened up the refrigeration unit and pulled out two sodas.

"This one's on me," he said, handing one to Chris.

"What happened back there?" Chris asked, a little shaken. "I thought it was just a friendly game."

"Those two have forty years between 'em. Hauling stuff around out here makes you hard. They probably figured you'd be an easy mark. The last thing they expected was some academy brat coming on board and taking their money."

Chris was about to be offended when he saw the laughter in Jerry's eyes. "I guess I should be a little more careful."

"Words to live by." Jerry smiled and clapped him on the shoulder. "Still, I rather enjoy seeing those two taken down a notch now and then."

CHAPTER 3

Ryan and Amie could tell they were nearing the control center. The hallway was now devoid of all plant life, and the few passersby were in uniform. They came to a gateway, but there was nobody guarding it. A sign on the wall said in large official letters: WARNING! YOU ARE ENTERING A SECURED AREA. NO WEAPONS OR IMAGE RE-CORDERS ALLOWED.

Just beyond the sign, on either side of the passageway, two mammoth doors were recessed into the walls. Ryan stopped.

"Atmospheric doors," he said, a little smugly. "I read about 'em. They're hydraulic. In case of explosive decompression these babies slam shut faster than you can say 'squish.'"

Amie noticed they were standing between the doors and instinctively moved ahead several steps. They walked on down the hallway past a series of six polymer windows, which were stronger than steel but transparent like glass. The view inside revealed several sections of the control center with technicians bustling about or seated at computer consoles, seeing to the smooth operation of the station.

Just past the windows, a queue of uniformed station personnel waited to enter the control center. The identification process required both a fingerprint scan and voice print.

Ryan watched the procedure with interest for a few moments and was about to move on when he noticed a familiar face near the end of the line.

"Look! It's that guy who was following us. Hey!"

The workers in line merely watched curiously as the little man bolted in the opposite direction. Ryan took off in hot pursuit.

"Hey, wait up!" Amie called, trying to catch her brother.

The man was fast, but there were no side passages to escape to, and Ryan was gaining on him. They passed the atmospheric doors on the far side of the control center and Amie began to trail behind. The passageway became more crowded, and soon they were dodging pedestrians. Ryan was within ten yards of the man when he cut to the right down a short passage.

Gasping for breath, Ryan plowed into a pedestrian. By the time he had regained his footing, the passageway was empty. Straight ahead was a blank alcove with a bench to one side, with no other exits and no sign of the man. Once again he seemed to have vanished into thin air.

Amie showed up a moment later. Though she was too out of breath to speak, the question on her face was obvious. "We lost him." Ryan said disgustedly. "This is too weird. We better tell Dad."

The conference broke for lunch just as Ryan and Amie found the conference hall. While there had been no more adventures, there were many interesting distractions along the way.

This was not the first time they had tried to find their parents in a crowd. Without a word, Amie scrambled up on her brother's shoulders. She scanned the crowd for several long seconds before she spotted her mother.

When they finally squeezed through the front of the crowd, Millie's face underwent a marvelous transformation as she smiled for the first time in three hours. The morning had been full of very technical information.

"What a pleasant surprise. You've come just in time for lunch."

Nathan was busily trying to find an excuse not to have lunch with a representative of the media who had come to cover the symposium. Mrs. Graham caught his eye and drew his attention to the children. He told the newsman that pressing business had just come up, and he would have to decline.

The noise in the conference room precluded any serious conversation, so Nathan signaled for his family to follow him. They walked behind the podium and found an entrance behind a thick curtain. The door opened easily to a narrow passage.

With the door shut, the silence was deafening. Nathan led them around the perimeter of the conference room wall, through a busy kitchen, and out into the main corridor. They quickly found a stairway to B deck and opted for a small sandwich shop.

"What a circus," Millie said, when they were seated.

Nathan had had his fill of small talk. He removed his glasses for a moment and smoothed his eyebrows.

"What brings you two here so soon?"

"We saw that man again!" Amie blurted before Ryan could answer.

"The same man you saw last night, Ryan?"

Ryan nodded. "He was following us this morning, and it started to give us the creeps, so we decided to lose him, which was no problem, but we bumped into him again by the control center, and this time we chased him, and we would have caught him, too, but he ran around this corner and just disappeared, poof, like into thin air."

"What do you mean, *disappeared?*" Nathan asked.

"I was right on his heels, chased him right into a dead end, but when I got there a few seconds later he just wasn't there."

"It sounds like we have a mystery on our hands," Nathan mused.

"Dad? He's not a ghost, is he?" Ryan asked. Slightly embarrassed, he hoped the question sounded like a joke.

Nathan opened his eyes wide and spoke in a sepulchral whisper. "I wasn't going to tell you this, but there is a legend. . . . "

"Nathan!" Millie gave a warning look.

Nathan laughed. "Of course he's not a ghost. But I sure would like to know who he is and what he's up to."

When the symposium let out late in the afternoon, Nathan and Millie were almost the first ones through the door. To their surprise, Ryan and Amie were waiting—red faced—outside.

Millie smiled. "You two look flushed. Where have you been? Not chasing that little man, I hope."

"We were at the low-gravity gymnasium. It's incredible! You've got to try it."

Laughing and talking, the Grahams walked to the nearest information booth. Nathan obtained the day's docking schedule, and the family headed off at a brisk pace to meet their missing member.

As the freighter approached the space station, Chris was in the cockpit again, watching Jerry work. With exaggerated ease and impressive fluidity of motion, Jerry's hands danced over the controls. Chris complimented him on his performance and Jerry smiled, but he never took his eyes off the controls.

"Compared to the army fighters I used to fly, this is kid stuff."

"You were in the Army?"

"Interplanetary Police Force."

"I hear that pays pretty good. Why aren't you still doing it?"

Jerry didn't answer, and Chris decided the query was best left alone. An uncomfortable silence ensued, broken at last by a curt order from one of the other crew members to find a seat. Chris made his way out of the cockpit and strapped himself in. He kicked himself for hurting Jerry's feelings, but he couldn't think of any way to repair his blunder.

The remainder of the trip passed in silence. Chris tried to turn his thoughts to happier things, like seeing his parents and tormenting his little brother and sister. The freighter docked without incident, and he hurried to the cargo hold, grabbed his bags, and made for the exit. As he passed the cockpit, he stuck his head in, said, "Thanks for the ride," and ducked out again without waiting for an answer. Somehow he figured this crew would not be big on long good-byes.

He walked off the ship into the landing bay and his family surrounded him. All the unpleasantness of the journey was quickly forgotten in a deluge of warm hugs and hearty hand-shakes.

After getting Chris settled in their quarters, the Grahams met Jacob Barber at a quiet restaurant for dinner. There, at a se-cluded table, Jacob talked about old times and pumped Chris with questions about the academy. When he heard they were all going on the tour of the accelerator the following day, he insisted on telling them the whole story about Dr. Graham, Dr. Mader, and the design fiasco. Nathan tried to shut him up, but the damage was already done. His family would not rest until they had heard all the gruesome details.

After Jacob had finished his story, Ryan still wasn't clear on a few details. "You said the project manager was replaced by Dr. Misenberg. Who was the first guy and what happened to him?"

Before Jacob could answer, a voice came from the shadows beside their table. "His name was Dr. Vorvick Shaw, and he is currently the administrator for this station."

Everyone at the table jumped, and a tall man with graying hair and kind eyes stepped out of the shadows. Jacob finally found his voice. "Wh . . . wh . . . Dr. Shaw, welcome. . . . I mean . . . what a pleasant surprise."

The tall man smiled. "Likewise. I didn't mean to eavesdrop. Forgive me for startling you, but when I spotted you over here I thought I should greet you personally. Nathan, I see you brought your beautiful family with you."

"Hello, Vick." Only Millie noticed the cool edge in her hus-band's voice. "Congratulations on your appointment. This is some place you have here."

"We're consistently rated in the top five stations in either solar system. Fortunately, I have a talented group of people working for me. I trust you're taking the tour of the accelerator tomorrow?"

"My family is. I have two more days to go at the symposium. But I want to thank you for your gracious hospitality."

"Not at all. It's an honor to have so many distinguished minds visit our humble station. If you'll excuse me, I must return to my guests." He turned and disappeared.

Silence reigned for a few moments. "He seems like a nice enough guy," Ryan said at last.

"Oh yes. And he's brilliant," Nathan said, still gazing at the spot where Dr. Shaw had been standing.

"Well, after all the mean things they did to him," Amie said, "he still has a nice smile."

"So does a crocodile, *Liebchen*."

Millie couldn't read the look on her husband's face, but she knew she didn't like it. "What have you got against Dr. Shaw?"

"After the accelerator was completed, I was reassigned, but Dr. Misenberg stayed on to oversee construction of the space station. Shortly after the station was completed, Dr. Misenberg disappeared. He was never heard from again, and I think Dr. Shaw had something to do with it."

The remainder of the meal passed in relative silence after that, although Jacob made several valiant efforts to get the conversation going again. After dinner, they walked around a bit and then Dr. Barber bade them goodnight. They stopped at an ice cream shop on the way back to their room, but it wasn't until they settled down in their quarters that Chris realized how tired he was.

"You know, I was only weightless for five days, but I'm really feeling sluggish."

"I always said you were a slug," Ryan said, entirely too pleased with his own pun.

"Watch your mouth, runt."

"All right, you two, knock it off." Millie was not about to

have her family time spoiled by petty bickering. "Chris, tell us more about your classes."

"Well, in my Applied Physics class they found out I was coming here, so I have to do a report on the accelerator a week after I get back."

"Which class do you enjoy the most?" Nathan wanted to know.

"That's easy. Propulsion Mechanics shop. We're building our own rocket bikes from scratch. At the end of the year we get to test 'em out."

His mother didn't like the sound of that. "Isn't that awfully dangerous?"

"Professor Estrom checks them out first from front to back. If he finds any problems with your bike, you fly it with a remote control."

The conversation ebbed for a moment. At last Nathan spoke.

"If I may change the subject: Chris, there's something I need to tell you. I was hoping this would be a simple vacation for all of us, but we've had something of a mystery develop. The day after we arrived we got a note telling us we were in danger and that we should leave. Since then, Ryan has noticed a man in station uniform watching us on several occasions."

"Why don't you ask him what he wants?"

"Ryan tried. He even chased him from the control center, but this fellow has a habit of disappearing into thin air. It may mean nothing, but it would probably be wise to keep your eyes open."

Chris smiled bemusedly. "Sounds interesting. Thanks for the heads up."

The "heads up" triggered Amie's memory. "Oh! I almost forgot."

She picked up a shoulder bag and rummaged inside, finally producing a gold medallion with an engraving of the station on the front.

"I bought this for you at a gift shop today," Amie said, presenting the packet to Chris.

Chris smiled, examining the medallion. It was an inch and a half across, plated with real gold. "Thanks, squirt. You didn't have to do that."

"I know. I wanted to be sure you knew you were missed."

"Thanks. I can tell," Chris replied, mussing her hair.

"The tour of the accelerator is tomorrow," Mrs. Graham reminded everybody. "It shouldn't take more than two or three hours, so maybe we could all get together for lunch."

"Since I'm going to be by myself, why don't I plan to meet you at the loading dock around noon?" Nathan suggested.

Ryan was looking forward to the tour, if for no other reason than he was tired of looking over his shoulder for that annoying little man in uniform.

Chris woke up at 5:30 the following morning, before anyone else was stirring. Carefully, he dressed and slipped out of the room. The air was surprisingly fresh and cool out in the hallway, and he stopped to breathe it in for a moment. Reaching into his pocket, he pulled out a map of the station given to him the previous evening by his brother. He chuckled as he noticed that Ryan had thoughtfully written "Slug" in the upper right corner so he would know which map was his.

None of the shops was open this early, but Chris didn't have shopping in mind this particular morning. The map was hard to read in the dim light of the hallway, but he found what he was looking for nonetheless. He folded the map and returned it to his pocket, then strode off to find the control center.

Fifteen minutes and two quadrants later, he entered the corridor adjacent to the control center. The lights were brighter here, as he passed the atmospheric doors and the windows of the control room; he could see a skeleton crew were at their stations. Then he was at the main entrance.

He looked both ways down the corridor and saw various official doors spaced unevenly along the walls. The closest one was thirty paces back the way he had come. Though recessed a few inches, it would not provide much of a hiding place. Well, it would just have to do. He remembered what his father had said about Ryan chasing the little man from here. With any luck, he would get a chance to talk to him.

Chris waited another quarter of an hour before station personnel began drifting one by one to the main entrance. He watched with interest the dual identification procedure and thought about how difficult it would be to get in without clearance. He studied each face intently, looking for some clue that might give away the man's identity. Suddenly, there was a hand on his shoulder. He whirled around in shock.

"I didn't know you were a pilot." It was Jerry.

"You scared the pants off me."

Jerry looked down. "Nope. Still there. Preppie, but there."

"What does *preppie* mean?"

"My grandpa told me that a long time ago academies were called 'prep schools.'"

"So it's not an insult."

Jerry thought for a moment and smiled. "Actually, it probably is."

"Thanks a bunch. What are you doing here?"

"Our cargo has been delayed a few days and we have to file a new flight plan." He indicated the sign on the door Chris had chosen: FLIGHT COORDINATOR.

Chris blushed at his own lack of observation. "Aren't you a little early?"

"I don't like to be late. What are you doing here?"

"Waiting for somebody." Chris glanced down the hallway once more.

"Oh. Here I was so impressed that you'd found out where I was going before I knew it myself. I thought maybe you were feeling guilty about leaving without saying good-bye."

"I said good-bye."

"'Thanks for the ride'?"

Chris blushed again. "Well, I felt bad about hurting your feelings."

"Listen. For starters, it's impossible to hurt a freighter pilot's feelings. I just didn't want to get too deep with the other guys around. I'd never hear the end of it."

"So why did you quit?"

"I watched a friend get blown up in a training exercise. You know what hotshots IPF pilots are. No one bothered to tell me I could get killed doing it."

"Couldn't get back on the horse?"

"Got back on the horse okay, but didn't enjoy it anymore."

Just then a man in uniform walked up, glanced at the two young men wordlessly, and then unlocked the door and went inside. The sound of the door closing reverberated briefly through the corridor, and all was quiet. Chris looked toward the entrance to the control center. Still no sign of the little man.

Jerry tapped him on the shoulder. "What are you doing on the station, anyway?"

"My dad had to come to a symposium."

"What's your dad do?"

"He's head of forensics for SAFCOM. He helped design the accelerator."

"Dr. Nathan Graham?"

"That's right. How'd you know?"

"You spend enough time out here, you hear just about everything that goes on. Not much else to do but talk between stops." Jerry checked the time. "Well, I got work to do. Looks like your friend's a no-show. You going to hang out for a while?"

"I'll give him another ten minutes. Good luck on your shipment."

"Thanks. I'll see you around."

They shook hands reluctantly, and Jerry entered the flight coordinator's office. Chris returned his attention to the main entrance, thinking about what it must have been like to be a military pilot. People were passing by more frequently, and he noticed that it was nearly 6:30. He was ready to give up when he saw him.

The man was easily a head shorter than anyone in the corridor and headed straight for the control room entrance. Chris left his hiding place, hoping to intercept the man before he reached the security panel beside the door. They were no more than ten steps apart when the man looked up. Realization seized his face and he turned and bolted like a scared jack rabbit. There was no question about it. Somehow, the man had recognized him.

Chris had not planned on chasing him down, but curiosity took over and he broke into a run. By the time he rounded the corner, the man had a fifty-foot head start. Judging by the stories from Ryan, if the man turned any corners, he would be gone. Chris poured on the speed and began closing the gap.

The man rounded a corner up ahead, and Chris growled "No!" through clenched teeth. He took the same corner without slowing down, careening off the wall and closing the gap. The man pulled up short in front of an access panel on a large pipe. Suddenly an opening appeared, and he scurried up a ladder inside.

The panel closed as Chris ran up, and he jammed his foot into the narrow opening that was left. Sensors in the panel responded and the panel slid open again. Chris stepped through onto the ladder and started climbing. The man was twenty feet up and moving fast, but Chris was gaining on him.

The gap had closed to ten feet when the man punched a button in the wall and stepped out onto another level. Chris scanned the surface for the controls and followed suit. The hallway was empty. Holding his breath, he listened and heard footfalls receding to the left.

Hot in pursuit, he rounded a corner in time to see two massive double doors closing. Chris slipped through with inches to spare and found himself ankle deep in mud. The little man was splashing through the mire up ahead.

The agricultural section ran 270 degrees around the circumference of the station, with plowed fields, crops, and grazing cattle. The farm seemed to stretch forever up out of sight around the curve of the station. The only part that didn't belong were the security guards by the granaries.

"Hey! What are you doing? Stop! I said, *Stop!*"

When Chris ignored their orders, the guards started after him. The little man dodged into a high corn patch and Chris plunged in after him. He could see nothing but plants. He stopped to listen and heard someone crashing through the corn ahead to his right. The guards had stopped also, listening for Chris, but he had come too far to give up now. He charged off through the corn again.

Suddenly he was out, and he could see the little man had lengthened his lead. There were agricultural workers farther on along the field, and it was clear from the depth of the soil that they had just plowed this part of the field. Chris pushed on, legs pumping madly, but his thighs were screaming from the effort of running through the mud. Eyes focused on the little man, he didn't see the narrow irrigation pipe protruding from the mud. One foot slipped neatly under the pipe and Chris plunged face first into the freshly tilled mulch.

The man reached the far wall, and Chris watched helplessly as another panel slid open and the man escaped. Once the panel shut, it was impossible to find the outlines of the door or the control mechanism.

"Blast!" Chris slapped his thigh and suddenly realized he was covered from head to foot with mud. Then he noticed people, angry people—guards to be exact—coming out of the corn behind him.

"Get off the tomatoes, kid."

Chris looked down. He was standing on a tomato plant.

With a guard at each arm, Chris was escorted back to his quarters. Nathan answered the door.

"What happened to you?"

59

"I was out running and took a wrong turn. I ended up in the agricultural section. Apparently that's a secured area."

The guards were actually being pretty nice about it, probably because of Nathan's reputation. "Next time, sign up for the tour."

Chris smiled apologetically, and the guards took their leave. Nathan led his son inside. "You need to get cleaned up, but before you do, what really happened?"

"I was chasing Ryan's mystery man. He's a squirrelly little guy."

Ryan walked up to his brother. "Nice outfit. Been out foraging for slug bait?"

"Come closer, little brother. You look like you need a hug."

Ryan took a step back and Nathan stepped between them. "Hit the showers. Ryan doesn't need your help to get filthy."

By the time Chris was cleaned up, the rest of the family was ready to go. He recounted the morning's adventure in the agricultural section, and after a prayer for the day, the family headed out the door for breakfast. By now all of them were famished.

About the only thing Jerry liked about Perimeter One Station was the food. On his way back from the flight coordinator's office, he decided to have a bite to eat, since it was the last real food he was likely to see for a while. A waffle shop caught his eye and he took an empty table by the front window.

Jerry sat back in his chair to wait for his breakfast and watch people. He was thinking about the philosophical differences between "regular" people and freighter pilots, when he saw something that drove every thought from his mind. Sten was walking the halls like a normal human being.

Seeing his ill-tempered crew member mingling with the rest of humanity was more than Jerry's curiosity could bear. He hurried out of the waffle shop and clapped a hand on Sten's shoulder. The thin man whirled around as if he were trapped, terror in his eyes.

"What do you want?" he sneered, but his voice was shaking.

"Relax. I just wanted to know what you're doing here."

"Why?"

"Because you hate people. And, on the whole, they hate you. What brings you on the station?"

"I . . . I was. . . ." Sten looked over Jerry's shoulder at the specialty food shops along the wall. "I was getting supplies."

"What kind of supplies?"

"Uh . . . food."

Jerry smelled a rat. "Where are these supplies?"

"Um . . . I'm having them delivered to the ship."

Sten was a lousy liar, but Jerry pretended not to notice. "Oh. Good thinking. Carry on."

Sten turned and snaked off through the crowd. Jerry wandered back to the waffle shop, wondering what mischief he was up to.

The Misenberg Accelerator was a uniquely monstrous construction 300 feet wide and 700 miles long. It had taken five years for a crew of ten thousand working round the clock to finish, and another two years of testing and tuning, before it was ready for operation.

From a distance, it looked like a giant pipeline, but upon closer inspection it was actually a long series of rings, spaced 100 feet apart. Each ring consisted of four sections of a special alloy joined by hexagonal metal housings twelve feet across. Each contained its own computer, megaplex signal splitter, generator, and retro rocket. The splitter isolated and maintained integrity for each communication signal. The generator served the dual purpose of energizing the rings and powering the rockets. The rockets automatically fired whenever a ring drifted more than 15 microns out of alignment.

The rings tapered slightly, beginning at a diameter of 300 feet and shrinking to 100 feet at the end. The rings were connected by thick cables to keep them aligned and to allow overall control by the main computer in the control module just beyond the first ring.

While the accelerator functioned in principle like late twentieth-century particle accelerators, it was designed to take incoming communication signals and increase their power logarithmically along a shallow time curve. The fields created by the ring generators created the electromagnetic equivalent of suction inside the accelerator, pulling in microscopic particles of dust and spewing them out the far end at high velocity.

The power increase to the millions of carrier waves entering the accelerator had to be slow enough to maintain the integrity of each signal. That's why there were 700 miles of rings, each slightly more focused, slightly more charged than the last.

On this particular morning it was business as usual in the control module for the accelerator. Technicians were preparing for the weekly three-minute cessation of incoming signals as the tourist barge performed its customary flyby. The tour was a nuisance, but they were used to it.

On board the barge in the VIP section, the four Grahams were waiting with some anticipation.

"I wish Dad could see this," Ryan said, looking out his window.

In the next seat, Chris never took his eyes off the approaching accelerator. "He helped design the thing. He hardly needs to see it again."

The barge was actually a converted cargo ship 75 feet wide and 150 feet long. Fully loaded, she seated 270 passengers and 5 crew. The captain was a bulky stump of a man, nearly as wide as he was tall. Seldom given to deep thought, it was he who had provided the appellation "barge" for his ship. He would have preferred not to name it at all, but registration required it. The other crew members referred to the ship—and sometimes the captain—as "The Tub," but not in his presence.

As the barge drew near, the accelerator became majestic in

appearance. The huge rings stretched off into the distance, with bright energy arcs glowing inside them.

Ryan was about to point this out to Chris when the captain's voice came over the public address system. "Good morning, ladies and gentlemen. This is your captain speaking. On our left, as you are no doubt already aware, is the Misenberg Accelerator, the communications conduit to the Jemini Solar System." He went on to describe the history of the accelerator and its construction as the barge moved closer to the gaping maw of the first ring, close enough that exhaust from the engine was being pulled into the accelerator.

Suddenly, Chris looked away from the window and frowned, listening. "The engines have stopped."

The captain's voice came over the PA system again, "Ladies and gentlemen, this is the captain. We seem to have lost our engines . . . just kidding. I like to give my passengers a little thrill for their money."

A wave of nervous laughter rippled through the cabin and people resumed their viewing of the accelerator. Chris was not amused and returned to his viewport.

In the command seat, the captain chuckled to himself, thinking about all those "tourists and their brats" quaking in their seats, if only for a few seconds. He initiated the start sequence as he had a thousand times before.

Nothing happened.

He tried it again. Still nothing.

Beads of perspiration formed on his upper lip. "Zane, we got a problem."

The copilot leaned over from his console and tried the start-up sequence himself, to no effect. Both men felt the gnawing grip of panic in their chests, even as the passengers began to wonder if something was wrong.

Chris looked at his mom. "They should have restarted by now. I'm gonna go see if there's trouble."

He left his seat, walked quickly up the aisle to the front of the cabin, and knocked on the door to the cockpit. When a second knock produced no answer, he peeked inside to find the captain and copilot frantically cross-circuiting the command console.

"What's the problem?" Chris asked.

The copilot was too frantic to be indignant at the intrusion. "Engines won't restart."

"I figured that much. Did you check the engines?"

"I do a level one diagnostic every time we take her out."

"Maybe you missed something."

At this point, the copilot was willing to try anything. He threw open a hatch in the floor. "Do you know anything about engines?"

"Some."

"Come on."

Chris followed him down the ladder to a long, narrow walkway made of metal grating, in what used to be the cargo hold. The walkway was suspended from the ceiling by metal cables and apparently ran the length of the ship.

The copilot took off running, with Chris close behind. They reached the end of the cargo hold and the walkway dead-ended into a door. In a moment they were through and desperately trying to locate the problem with the engines. The copilot began by digging into the electrical relays.

Chris examined the injector housing. "Did you check the injectors?"

"I told you I checked everything."

Chris opened a toolbox, pulled out a large hex-head wrench, and went to work on the bolts anchoring the faceplate for the injector housing.

The copilot shot a quick glance in his direction, but went on with his search. "You're wasting your time. I told you I checked everything."

"You find any electrical problem?"

"No."

"Then the first thing I'd check is the injectors."

The copilot thought for a moment, then pulled out another hex-head wrench and went to work beside Chris. In thirty seconds they had the faceplate off, revealing a small pile of molten slag.

"That's impossible. The main injector's been deliberately fused!" the copilot said.

Chris poked around in the debris, careful to touch nothing else. "Looks like a Y-trigger switch."

"You mean it was armed when we started the engines?"

"And triggered when the captain shut them off."

"Well, it wasn't here when I did my preflight check. Whoever did this had to have clearances."

"Do you have a spare?"

"This isn't an interstellar cruiser, kid. We don't have a lot of money for spare parts."

"Well, this is beyond repair. Looks like we're going to need a tow back to the station."

They left the faceplate and tools on the floor and ran out the door, headed for the cockpit. On the walkway, they nearly ran into the captain. He was moving toward them as fast as his girth would allow, his face red with the effort. "Do we have our engines back?"

"No chance," the copilot replied. "Main injector's fused."

"We're being pulled into the accelerator."

Chris and the copilot squeezed around the captain and scrambled up into the cockpit. It was true. Their forward momentum had stopped and they were drifting slowly, inexorably toward the opening of the accelerator.

"Nose around!" the copilot yelled.

The captain activated the positional thrusters and slowly turned the barge until it was pointing directly into the accelerator. The copilot was leaning over the captain's shoulder. "Use port side thrusters at full power. Maybe we can get clear of this thing."

Chris knew instinctively that there was something dreadfully wrong with the plan. "Wait. How many port side thrusters do you have?"

"Two rated at sixteen thousand foot pounds per second."

"How far are we from the accelerator?"

"Fifty-four feet."

"What's our closing speed?"

"We're at one-point-eight-seven miles per hour."

"What does the barge weigh?"

"Eighty thousand metric tons. Are you finished yet?"

Chris ignored him and did some quick mental calculations. "We'd never make it past the first ring."

"You got a better suggestion?"

"Keep it as straight as you can and pray."

In the accelerator control room there was pandemonium. "She's going in, she's going in!" a technician yelled from his console.

The commander slammed his hand down on a table and growled, "I knew this would happen. We never should have given that buffoon a permit. General alarm—Code One."

The technician popped the safety of a large red button on his control panel and pressed the button with his thumb. Red lights and alarms went off everywhere.

On the station, Dr. Vorvick Shaw charged out of his office and across the floor to the communications console. "That's a Code One! What happened?"

"As near as we can tell, the passenger barge got pulled into the accelerator."

The blood drained from Dr. Shaw's face. "Any casualties?"

"Not yet. She's still in one piece. Apparently the pilot got her nosed around before she went in."

"Send a Priority One distress call to Perimeter Command and get someone to the conference hall before this gets out and we have a riot on our hands."

CHAPTER 4

In the conference hall, Nathan sat with the rest of his colleagues listening to a dry dissertation about advances in subatomic metallurgy. He checked to be sure he had all the handouts and was seriously considering a break, when an attractive woman in a lab coat ran down the center aisle to the front. Something about the look on her face put Nathan's stomach in a knot.

"Ladies and gentlemen, please forgive the interruption, but I have some important news to give you and I need your undivided attention. I will be happy to answer any questions when I'm through. At ten-seventeen this morning, the passenger barge touring the Misenberg Accelerator lost engine power. The command crew was unable to restart the engines and the barge drifted nose first into the accelerator. At present there have been no injuries reported, but the barge is travelling at two-point-four miles per hour and picking up speed. A Priority One distress call has been issued and emergency contingency plans are under evaluation.

"To avoid confusion and to help us keep you informed, please remain in this room until further notice. You will only impede our progress if you try to crowd the control center, so please remain here. The following people are requested to return with me to the control center. Dr. Nathan Graham . . ."

Nathan didn't wait to hear the rest of the list, but exited the hall and ran down the corridor to the control center. He pounded on the nearest window until Dr. Shaw recognized him and told one of the technicians to let him in.

"Vick, what happened?"

"The barge always cuts her engines as she flies by the front of the accelerator to make the trip a little more exciting. The passengers have always enjoyed it and we never have had a problem, so we tolerated it. This time the engines didn't restart."

"My family's on that barge."

"I know. I need your help on this one, Nathan, but if you don't think you can be objective. . . ."

Nathan ignored the insult. "We need to establish communication with the barge."

"We lost communications as soon as she went into the accelerator."

"I expected that. They'll be trying to contact us. Start scanning low frequencies. It's the only way they'll be able to get a signal out. Also, I'll need the full text of the Accelerator Specifications Manual."

On the barge, the copilot, two stewards and a stewardess were filtering among the passengers, answering frantic questions and urging everyone to keep their wits about them. In the cockpit, the captain and Chris were trying unsuccessfully to raise the station on the communicator.

The captain set the headset down in disgust. "It's interference from the rings, I tell you. They can't hear us."

"We have to find a way to get through. I don't suppose you have anyone trained in communications electronics."

The captain shook his head. Chris exited the cockpit and nearly bumped into the copilot. He asked him how the passengers were.

"Calm for the moment."

"Have you got a minute?"

He followed Chris back to his seat and sat down opposite Mrs. Graham, who looked at her son curiously. Chris introduced his mother, brother, and sister. Ryan and Amie smiled vaguely at the stranger and then decided to ignore the interruption and continue staring out the window. Chris looked from his mother to the copilot. This was going to be like one of his team meetings in propulsion mechanics class.

"We got a problem. As soon as we entered the accelerator we lost communications. The captain thinks it's interference from the rings and I agree. We need to communicate with the station. What are our options?"

The copilot looked thoughtful. "Try to boost the signal."

"How?" Chris asked.

"We'd have to take the console apart and tap into the main power grid without frying the circuits or one of us."

"You care to try it?"

The copilot shook his head.

Millie spoke up. "We could try to modulate the frequency."

Chris looked at his mom in surprise. He knew she had some technical credentials in her background, but she rarely talked business at home. The copilot considered her suggestion but shook his head again. "We'd have to pull the communications circuit boards and try to reprogram some of the chips. Impossible without a schematic."

Chris was incredulous. "You don't have frequency control from the panel?"

"This is an old cargo ship. Fixed frequency. The captain bought it on sale at a government auction."

"Great. What else do you have that could possibly send a signal?"

"There's a distress beacon, but it only sends and receives low frequency pulses."

"Is there any way to patch voice communications through the distress beacon?"

"No. We'd still need a schematic of the circuit board."

Silence took over as each member of the little group was

deep in thought. After a few moments, Mrs. Graham's face brightened.

"Excuse me, but I don't know your name."

"I'm Zane. I'm one of the idiots responsible for your current predicament."

"He's the copilot, Mom."

"Zane, do you have a navigation computer?"

"It's pretty basic. We haven't had to use it much."

"Does it have a standard keyboard?"

"Sure."

"I want to see it." Mrs. Graham was on her feet and up the aisle before anyone could say anything. Zane and Chris exchanged a look, then followed her. By the time they reached the cockpit, she had already disconnected the keyboard from the computer.

"May I ask what this woman is doing?" the captain roared.

Zane put a hand on his shoulder to calm him down. "Testing a theory, I think."

"Well, get her somewhere else, will you? I have my hands full keeping this heap straight."

Mrs. Graham handed the keyboard to Chris. "I could plug this into any computer and it would work, right?" she asked rhetorically.

"Just about. You can still find some nonstandard systems out there."

"Is there any reason you couldn't hook this up to the distress beacon and send messages one character at a time?"

"We might be able to hook it up, but even assuming they're scanning low frequencies, how would they know what we're saying? The characters would arrive as an analog signal."

"They'd have to figure it out. We could send the same message until they respond."

"How will we know what they're saying?"

"If we hook the receiving end of the beacon to the computer,

70

and they use the same code the keyboard is sending, wouldn't an analog-to-digital converter allow the computer to read it?"

"It sounds like a long shot."

"Do you have a better idea?"

"Not at the moment."

"Then I'd get to work on it. Assuming it meets with Zane's approval."

"Okay by me. At least it will give us something to do."

Millie turned and started to leave, but Zane stopped her. "Mrs. Graham, how did you learn so much about computers?"

Her eyes twinkled briefly. "I wasn't always a mother, you know."

Nathan sat reading a dog-eared manual at the communications console in the space station control center, while the comm chief stretched his legs nearby. He'd skimmed thirty chapters but was only about a quarter of the way through the book. Finally he stood up.

"Here it is. A table of all the rings, their diameters, and power consumption specs. There are forty thousand rings total, but at least we'll be able to know what they're up against as we track their position."

The comm chief sat back down in his seat and looked at the monitor in disgust. Still nothing.

Nathan tried to push the worry from his mind. "Once they hit the five hundred mile mark they're going to need shielding from the energy arcs. It's going to be hard enough to steer the barge without having holes punched in her hull."

"Where are they going to get shielding?" Dr. Shaw asked.

"Someone will have to take it to them."

"I can't authorize that. It would be suicide."

"Unless you have a ship big enough to catch them and tow them out, what other chance have they got?" Nathan looked around the room, hoping for support. No one said anything.

"Vick, do you have any small ships fast enough to catch the barge?"

"How fast is she traveling right now?"

A uniformed officer at another console checked his instruments. "Twenty miles per hour, and accelerating."

Dr. Shaw turned to Nathan with something akin to pity in his eyes. "By the time we got one loaded and out there, it would be too late."

"There has got to be a way."

"I'm sorry, Nathan. I wish there were something I could do."

Nathan wondered about the sincerity of that wish, as he sat next to the comm chief and began digging through the manual once more.

In another part of the station, Jerry was striding briskly toward his freighter with his new flight plan in hand. There was a spring in his step and he whistled cheerily to himself, mostly because he was looking forward to getting away from the crowds of tourists.

He walked across the small landing bay and onto the freighter without looking back. His two shipmates were there, but something was different about them—something that made the hair stand up on the back of his neck. Griff was standing by the door to the cockpit. Jerry turned and saw that Sten had moved around behind, blocking his exit.

"H'lo, Jerry," Griff said flatly around his cigar.

Sten looked nervous. "We've been waiting for you."

Jerry smiled his most disarming smile and said, "Well, here I am. Have you started the preflight check?"

Griff motioned toward the cockpit. "We're having trouble keeping pressure."

"Let's have a look," Jerry said, all of his senses on full alert.

He stepped past Griff into the cockpit, bending over the console as if looking for a problem. The pressure was fine, and Jerry looked up. Reflected in the window, he saw Sten walk in quietly with an object in his hands and the glint of metal from Griff's direction. Jerry punched the communicator, and the two men froze.

"Control, this is NK7544. Looks like we're ready to launch."

A voice came over the communicator. "Roger that. Depressurizing the launch bay."

Jerry turned and looked both men in the eye. "Well? Don't just stand there. Take your seats."

At the word *seats*, Jerry swung his fist over Sten's shoulder, connecting solidly with Griff's face. The big man's head hit the wall, but he didn't go down, and Sten pushed Jerry onto the console, pressing a metal pipe against his throat.

Catching a glimpse of the knife in Griff's hand, Jerry grabbed Sten's wrists and pushed him backward. Griff hit the wall again, and Jerry twisted out of the way, as Sten brought the pipe down in a vicious arc. The pipe struck a glancing blow above Jerry's right eye.

Sten raised the pipe again, but Jerry thrust his open palm into Sten's face. The man reeled back into the bulkhead, holding his nose with both hands. Jerry turned just in time to dodge a knife thrust from Griff, who stumbled as he passed and nearly collided with his wounded comrade.

The two men were tangled up with each other, momentarily draped over the pilot's chair, and Jerry ran for the exit. In the cockpit, Griff slammed his fist down on the emergency lock controls, sealing off any escape. Fear welling up inside his chest, Jerry turned and ran down the hallway toward the cargo hold, hoping to find something to use as a weapon.

He lunged into the hold, aware of the heavy footsteps behind him, desperately trying to figure out how he was going to survive. Blood from the gash on his forehead was making it hard to see. Looking from side to side, his heart sank as he saw that everything in the hold was either crated up or tied down.

The cargo bay doors looked like the only way out, but the

landing bay was depressurized by now. He wouldn't last long without an environment suit.

Griff and Sten clattered into the cargo hold and stopped as they caught sight of their prey. They knew he was cornered.

"Don't make this any harder than it already is," Griff said, brandishing the knife. Sten was holding the pipe with one hand and still holding his nose with the other.

"Why do you guys want to kill me?" Jerry asked, backing toward the bay doors.

"We're using our heads, Jerry, just like you told us," Griff sneered.

Sten seemed almost apologetic. "Don't take it personal. This is just business."

"We came into some big money," Griff added.

Sten bared his teeth in a weasel's grin. "You're a smart guy, Jerry. We figured you'd ask a lot of embarrassing questions about where we got it."

Jerry had run out of room. "Can't we make a deal?"

There was death in Griff's eyes. "You don't have anything we want."

Jerry looked down and saw a metal pry bar between two stacks of boxes. He picked up the metal bar and held it like a baseball bat.

Sten took a step backward, but Griff just laughed. He reached inside his jacket and pulled out a laser pistol.

"I was afraid the security guys on the station might pick up a blast from this thing. I guess I'll just have to take that chance."

"You pull that trigger and you're a dead man," Jerry said evenly.

Griff's smile faded. "I think you got that backwards."

"These crates are filled with trimagnasite. One shot from a laser, and the whole cargo hold goes up in a fireball."

Griff reconsidered, then stuck the pistol back inside his jacket.

"Guess we'll have to do this the hard way," he growled.

Both men advanced. Sten was hanging back, hoping Griff

would be able to finish the job. As the big man moved in, Jerry lunged and swung with the pry bar. Griff sidestepped the blow and grabbed the bar, pulling Jerry toward him.

Jerry had underestimated Griff's strength badly. He was off balance and stumbling forward, while Griff stood ready with the knife. As he stepped within reach of the blade, Jerry dropped to the floor, clamped Griff's feet between his legs, and rolled, throwing Griff face down to the floor. Sten tried to pin Jerry to the floor, but Jerry scrambled to his feet and made for the door. Griff maneuvered sideways and blocked his way. Jerry backed up once again toward the cargo bay doors, and once again ran out of room.

"C'mon, Griff. I don't care what kind of business you run on the side," Jerry said, gingerly slipping his arm through a rope holding a large crate to the wall.

"Sorry, Jerry. You're a decent guy. Decent guys can't be trusted."

"I'll give you the freighter. You can leave me on the station, and I won't tell a soul."

"You got the last part right. Good-bye, Jerry."

Griff lurched forward with the knife, but Jerry twisted out of reach and the knife sank into the crate. He grabbed the rope with his other hand and kicked both feet into Griff's chest, knocking him to the floor. Jerry reached for the knife, but it wasn't there. Somehow, impossibly, Griff had jerked it out of the crate when he fell.

Sten stepped forward and swung wildly with the pipe, landing one or two glancing blows to Jerry's ribs. Griff was lumbering toward him again, knife in hand.

Still holding the rope, veins pumping with adrenaline, Jerry had an inspiration. He lashed out with his foot, catching Sten in the knee. Sten stumbled backward, but didn't go down. As Jerry's foot hit the deck, he shut his eyes tight, took a deep breath, and swung his right fist into the controls beside the bay doors. There was a mad rush of air as the doors flew open, sucking crates, Griff, and Sten out through the landing bay and into space.

With the explosive decompression of the cargo hold, the door to the hallway closed automatically. Jerry groped for the control panel frantically closing the bay doors. By the time they swung shut, his lungs were screaming for oxygen, though air was whistling into the hold from the ventilation system. He untangled his arm from the rope and staggered like a drunken sailor toward the door to the hallway. He punched the emergency open button and was knocked to the floor as air rushed into the cargo hold, equalizing the pressure.

Jerry lay on the deck, gasping in great lungfuls of air and trying to ignore the painful ringing in his ears. As his thinking cleared, he decided the next step would be to report the incident to station security. He worked his way to his feet and started down the hallway. Suddenly he fell against the wall and was violently ill.

The communicator in the cockpit was beeping, and he stumbled the rest of the way to the cockpit, leaning on the controls.

"Yeah."

"This is control. What happened in there?"

"Repressurize. I'm coming out."

Holding his side, he limped toward the exit. He caught a glimpse of himself in a mirror as he passed one of the storage closets. If anyone was going to take him seriously, he'd better clean himself up first.

Ten minutes later, he looked presentable, although he still felt a little woozy. He walked to the nearest security station, which happened to be the main security shuttle bay. Convincing the guard that this was an emergency, he stepped into the small bay control room and found two overweight men lounging in office chairs. He peeked out the window into the bay, just to see what kind of ships they had on deck. The nearest man looked up.

"What do you want?"

"I need to report an emergency. Two of my shipmates just got blown out into space."

"Were they wearing environment suits?"

"No."

"Then they're dead."

"I know that. I thought you might want to pick up the bodies."

"Listen, pal, we don't do anything without a direct order from the security office."

Jerry looked at their substantial waistlines. "I believe you. Where are the pilots?"

"We're the pilots."

Jerry realized the look of shock on his face was probably insulting, so he left hurriedly. At the security office, he was surprised to find everyone rushing about yelling orders into communicators. He wondered how they had discovered the untimely demise of his shipmates so quickly. Completely ignored, he finally snagged a passing officer.

"Excuse me, but I need to report an accident."

"If you're talking about the barge, we already know."

"No, I'm talking about . . . what about the barge?"

"She lost her engines. Pulled into the accelerator."

The officer hurried off, but Jerry didn't notice. His mind was occupied with one thought: *Chris*. He ran from the security office and found the nearest information booth. There a large group of people were clamoring for news about the barge.

Jerry put on his best military voice and barked, "Police business! Make way!"

Like magic a path opened to the counter, and he strode up to the attendant.

"Is there a Chris Graham on the roster for the barge?"

The attendant scanned the list on her monitor. "I only show a Mrs. Millie Graham, but she reserved four seats."

"Can you tell me the location of Dr. Nathan Graham?"

The attendant looked apologetic. "I have no way of knowing, but my best guess would be the conference hall."

From the conference hall Jerry finally tracked Nathan to the control center. Through the windows he could see several men engaged in a heated argument, and decided it was better not to interrupt. Instead he walked down the hall to the flight coordinator's office, the only room on the station that wasn't a flurry of activity.

The coordinator smiled at him over a sheaf of papers. "I thought you'd be long gone by now. What can I do for you?"

"Could you call into the control center? I need to talk to Dr. Graham."

The coordinator thought for a moment, then picked up the communicator, punched a few numbers, and handed him the device. "You go ahead. And don't say where you're calling from."

"Thanks. I really appreciate . . . hello? Dr. Graham, please."

Nathan came on the line. "This is Nathan Graham."

"Do you have a son named Chris?"

Nathan feared the worst. "Who is this?"

"My name is Jerry Wysoski. I piloted the freighter your son came in on."

The voice on the other end was noticeably relieved. "What can I do for you?"

"I struck up something of a friendship with your son during the trip, and I just wanted to let you know I'd be happy to help any way I can."

"You say you're a pilot?"

"Yes."

"Where are you right now?"

"Just down the hall." The coordinator glanced up from his papers but said nothing.

"Why don't you come to the control center? I'll let you in. We could use a fresh perspective."

Jerry handed the communicator back to the coordinator. "Thanks again."

"Don't mention it. Please."

He reached the control center entrance as Nathan was opening the door.

"Nathan Graham," he said, offering his hand.

Jerry shook it warmly. "Jerry Wysoski."

They walked into the control room, where they were met with mostly blank stares and one or two nods from the men and women gathered in the room. Nathan addressed the group in general.

"This is Jerry. He's a pilot. Jerry, when you called, we were in the process of trying to come up with an option for getting shielding to the barge before it picks up too much speed."

"What's the shielding for?"

"As you get closer to the end of the accelerator, the rings are smaller and there are increasing numbers of high energy arcs inside the rings. A direct hit could breach the hull."

"What kind of shielding do you need?"

"Reflective chromaluminum will work. The station has a large supply in stock."

"Why can't you just shut the accelerator down?"

"We've initiated an emergency shutdown, but it takes thirty-six hours. If we simply shut the power off, the rings will explode. When current isn't running through them, they store energy. We have to bleed the energy off slowly or we get an overload."

"How are you going to get the shielding to the barge?"

"That's what we were arguing about when you called. Dr. Shaw says we don't have any ships small enough and fast enough to catch the barge."

"I saw an IPF Fighter in the security bay."

Nathan shot an accusatory look at Dr. Shaw, who replied defensively, "We don't have anyone to fly it."

Jerry snorted. "He's right about that. I've seen their pilots."

"What do you use it for, then?"

"Traffic control, mostly."

"Then we really don't have a pilot."

"I can fly it," said Jerry matter-of-factly.

The entire room was suddenly still.

"I appreciate the offer, but flying a freighter is a little different."

"I started out as an IPF Fighter pilot."

"Why'd you quit?"

"Personal reasons. It doesn't matter. I'm telling you I can fly it."

Objections came from around the room, but Nathan shouted them all down. "If anyone has a better idea, now is the time." No one spoke. "With your permission, Dr. Shaw, I recommend we load the fighter with shielding and commission Jerry to take it to the barge."

Every eye was on Dr. Shaw. He waved his hand noncommittally at Nathan. "Suit yourself. But it's your responsibility."

CHAPTER 5

Millie Graham sat quietly in her seat, looking pensively out the window at the rings rushing past. She had noticed they were picking up speed and wondered how things were progressing in the cockpit.

"Mom, are we going to die?" Amie asked.

She thought about giving her a reassuring answer beginning with "Of course not," but there was something about the look on her daughter's face that demanded honesty.

"I don't know, dear. But I do know that God can save us if He wants to."

Amie was silent for a moment. "I hope He wants to."

Millie smiled. "Me too."

She squeezed her daughter's shoulder and then went forward to check on her older son. Chris and Zane were sitting on the floor of the cockpit, surrounded by faceplates, circuit boards, and an assortment of cables. Chris had needle-nosed pliers in one hand and tweezers in the other, and he was looking a little lost.

"How's it going?" Millie asked cheerfully.

"Well, I got the keyboard spliced to the send cable for the beacon. I haven't tested it, but that was fairly easy. Now I'm trying to hook up the receive cable to the monitor sub-assembly, but I've never worked with mnemonic circuits before."

Concentrating hard, Millie thought back seventeen years to

her working days, but drew a blank. "Lord, help me remember," she said under her breath.

She crouched down next to Chris and gazed into the nightmare of wires and circuits laid open in front of her son. Suddenly there was a picture in her head, like a photograph right out of a textbook.

"The signal from the beacon needs to be digitized so the computer can read it. Do you have a soldering iron?"

Zane raised his head and nodded. Millie closed her eyes. "Take cutters and clip off the connector at the end of the receive cable. Somewhere along the front of the computer, there should be a micro-voice input."

Chris was on his back, looking up into the computer. "Got it."

"There should be cables running in and out of a small box connected to the voice input. Disconnect and remove it."

He worked quietly for a moment and produced a small rectangular box. "This looks like an analog-to-digital converter."

"Yes. Now all we have to do is use this as a bridge between the receive cable and the mnemonic circuit for the monitor sub-assembly."

"Piece of cake," Chris said dryly.

As mother and son worked on the connections, Millie found her training coming back to her. They finished the job sometime later, though the work seemed to go very quickly. Chris thanked his mom and she took her leave. He and Zane stood up to stretch, noticing for the first time the mess they had made.

"It looks like somebody tore this apart," Chris mused.

"You did. Let's just hope it works."

They put everything back together again and powered it up, being sure not to stand too close in case the console went up in smoke. No flames were evident, and shortly a cursor appeared on the monitor. Cautiously optimistic, Chris sat down with his fingers over the keyboard.

"What should I type?"

"How about something simple, like 'S.O.S.—Station Do You Read?'"

Chris started typing. "So I just keep on until they answer?"

"That's right."

"What if they never answer?"

"Then you're going to be doing a lot of typing."

Perimeter One Station was now several hours into the crisis, and the comm chief was bored. He was doodling on the cover of a manual, when he thought he heard something. *Just static*, he thought to himself, but the pattern repeated itself. Quickly he adjusted the attenuator, and the signal became stronger. Then he noticed the frequency.

"I got something coming in on a distress frequency."

Nathan jumped up from a nearby chair. "Put it on speakers."

The control center listened to the burst of static coming over the speakers. Nathan broke into a grin.

"They've done it! Now all we have to do is decode the signal."

The comm chief was skeptical. "They could be using any of a thousand codes."

"You said they were on a distress frequency. It has to be an analog signal. If you were trying to send a message like that what code would you use?"

"Standard GSAL, but I'd have to have a keyboard with an A-to-D converter to do it."

"Can you punch up the signal in a graphic format on your screen?"

"No problem."

The comm chief typed in a series of commands, touched the screen in several places, and a graph appeared on the monitor.

"Great. Now, take out everything except the peak for each data point."

The comm chief made the necessary modifications to the chart, creating a very orderly series of points across the upper midsection of the graph.

Nathan was excited. "Look familiar?"

"It is GSAL!"

"Can you convert the signal?"

"I'll have to write a short program. But if we're going to respond in kind, I have some serious work to do." He picked up his communicator and punched in some numbers. "Jeffries, get up here with my toolbox and bring the spec manual for the comm console."

Chris's fingers were tiring. He typed the message one more time and gave up in frustration. "It's been almost an hour. It must not be working."

Zane was in the copilot's seat; the captain still at the helm. The captain glanced over his shoulder. "You gave it your best shot."

Chris was not satisfied. "It should have worked."

He looked out the front window and noticed for the first time just how breathtaking the view was. The rings were going by at the rate of one per second. "How much distance between each of the rings?"

"Hundred feet."

"So we're doing seventy miles per hour?"

"Sixty-eight."

The conversation was cut short as an energy arc seared past the front of the barge, narrowly missing her. Chris and Zane almost fell out of their seats, while the captain ducked, keeping his hands glued to the controls.

"That was close," Zane said.

"Is your hull shielded?" Chris asked, shaken.

"Nope. A direct hit will come right through."

"Do your seats meet interplanetary standards?"

The captain didn't look around. "Of course. I got 'em off a decommissioned cruiser."

"You might want to tell your passengers how to use them."

The captain grudgingly acquiesced, handing a grubby little

84

booklet and the PA communicator to Zane, who thumbed to the right page and began to read.

"Ladies and gentlemen, this is your copilot speaking. We are in no immediate danger, but in the event of a hull breach, each of your seats is equipped with seat cushions that meet or exceed interplanetary rift occlusion standards. If you notice a gap in the hull, remove your seat cushion and turn it sideways, taking hold of the handles on the bottom with both hands. Center the cushion with the top down over the gap and push it firmly into place. Under all other circumstances, please remain seated with your seatbelts fastened."

He stowed the booklet and communicator. "Well, that was exciting."

The captain spoke again. "Listen, kid, not that I don't appreciate your effort, but if we make it through this, I'm going to need my computer. Would you mind putting it back together?"

Chris turned back to the computer to switch it off and let out a whoop. There on the screen, repeated three times, was the message: STATION CONTROL—WE READ YOU.

"We got 'em!"

Nathan and Dr. Shaw rushed with the others to the communications console while the comm chief read the message aloud. "Main engines out. Can't repair. Thrusters only. Ship is eighty thousand metric tons. Speed seventy miles per hour and increasing. Thrust is thirty-two thousand f-p-s each side. Please advise."

Nathan spoke. "Okay, send this message: Increasing danger from arcs. Inform passengers. Sending shielding on fighter soonest. May need help with install. Ring interior diameter down to one hundred feet by end. Expect rough ride."

The group around the console waited impatiently as the message was received on the other end. The reply was quite unexpected

"PRIVATE MESSAGE FOR DR. GRAHAM FROM HIS SON."

The group politely dispersed and Nathan sat down at the console to type.

"THIS IS DR. GRAHAM."

"DAD—CHRIS HERE," the screen flashed back. "ARE YOU ALONE?"

"YES."

"SHIP SABOTAGED. PROBABLY INSIDE JOB. WATCH YOUR BACK."

Nathan was careful not to show any expression on his face as he typed back, "WILL DO. YOU TOO."

He cleared the screen and returned the seat to the comm chief. He announced to the control room that his family was doing well, then left to see how Jerry was coming along.

The fighter in the security bay looked more like a patient in a hospital bed than a sophisticated piece of machinery. Various tubes and hoses were attached here and there, and the shielding that had been secured to the outside of the fuselage looked like a thick bandage. Nathan found Jerry already suited up and lying under the belly of the fighter giving instructions to a technician.

"How's it going?"

"Good. We're twenty minutes from launch."

"Can I talk to you for a moment?"

Jerry crawled out from under the ship and followed Nathan to the far side of the bay.

"We made contact with the barge. Everyone's okay." Jerry nodded. "Chris told me the ship was sabotaged, probably by somebody with clearance. You might want to doublecheck the fighter."

"I supervised the preflight check myself, but I'll keep my eyes open."

As Nathan and Jerry continued their conversation, neither of them noticed a technician—wearing a work suit that was slightly too large—slip under the front of the fighter and attach a small device to the left side of the ship.

* * *

In the passenger cabin of the barge, things were settling down to a routine of sorts. Though tense, many people were reading or playing games. The stewards and stewardess had rationed out the small reserve of snacks and drinks, attempting to provide at least the illusion of normalcy.

The illusion was shattered a moment later, when an energy arc blew a hole in the hull. The hole was small, but the explosion was deafening. Shards of metal rained down on the passengers immediately below, followed by the smell of burnt synthetics. People were screaming, but their voices were drowned out by the unmistakable high-pitched whistle of atmosphere escaping.

A tall young man scrambled out of his seat and jerked his seat cushion out. Holding it by the handles, he stood on the armrest and jammed the cushion into the hole. On impact, the cushion liquified and then resolidified. The whistling stopped. There was scattered applause for his quick thinking.

Mrs. Graham, Ryan, Amie, and several other passengers began administering first aid to the injured passengers, many of them in shock. Fortunately, most of the injuries appeared to be minor.

Chris ran down the aisle to see if his family members were all right and was greatly relieved to find them busily at work, without a scratch on them. He returned to the cockpit to continue monitoring the computer for transmissions. The captain was still at the controls, with Zane trying to assist.

Chris sat down at the computer. "We took a hit at midship."

"That's what I thought. Any casualties?" the captain asked, still wrestling to regain control of the ship.

"Mostly lacerations. Some guy plugged the hole almost immediately."

"He should get a medal. You going to tell the station?"

Chris started typing. "Yeah. That shielding better get here soon."

Jerry was in the cockpit of the fighter, running through the final prelaunch check. Everything checked out and the control room gave him clearance to take off. The technical crew cleared the area and the security bay was depressurized.

Nathan's voice came over the headset in his helmet. "Jerry, this is Nathan. The barge was just hit by an energy arc. Some people were hurt. They closed a breach in the hull, but we're almost out of time."

The bay doors opened, Jerry keyed in the launch sequence, and the fighter's engines roared to life.

The fighter shot silently out into the vacuum of space, making a wide parabolic arc in the direction of the accelerator. In less than a minute the rings were in view. Jerry activated the communicator in his helmet.

"This is . . ." he looked at the signature plate on the control panel, "alpha-niner-niner tango fox 415. Do you copy?"

"This is station control, TF415. We read you."

"I need speed and distance to the barge."

"She's travelling at one-thirty-three miles per hour. Distance is two-eighty miles."

"I am on approach. Request authorization to enter the accelerator."

"TF415, this is flight control giving you authorization to proceed into the accelerator."

"I'm going in."

The fighter swung wide, jets blazing, and came in straight toward the mouth of the accelerator.

"TF415, this is accelerator control. You're coming in too fast."

Jerry ignored the warning, nudging the throttle forward a bit more.

"Repeat. TF415, you are coming in too . . ." The message

ended in an expletive as the fighter screamed past the accelerator control room and into the accelerator.

Jerry checked his speed. Just over 700 mph. He should catch the barge in about half an hour. He smiled for a moment, thinking about the control operator's reaction to his sudden arrival. The same stunt in an oxygen atmosphere would have blown their windows out.

The rings were going by so fast that he seemed to be flying down an amber tunnel. The electromagnetic fields made most of his instruments unreadable, so he kept his eyes front, checking the time every half minute or so. He noticed his speed picking up, and throttled back to compensate.

At fifteen minutes in, he switched to a low frequency and reported to the station that all was well, although the ride was getting rougher. At twenty minutes he throttled back to 350 mph and strained to see any sign of the barge ahead. He caught a glimpse of something ahead and throttled back even further. He was glad he had, as he came up on the rear of the barge very quickly.

"Station control, this is TF415. I have the barge in sight."

Chris was staring out the front window, while Zane continued his ongoing fight for control of the barge. So far, he'd done an admirable job of keeping her on course.

Chris glanced at the monitor. "Message coming in . . . there's a fighter behind us carrying shielding. It's going to land on the top rear of the barge. He'll be using hydraulic cleats to secure the ship to the outer hull. It will sound pretty awful so you better warn the passengers. The pilot is going to need help deploying the shielding. Do you have an environment suit?"

"A couple."

"Tell me where they are so I can suit up."

"Sorry, Chris. Technically, you're still a passenger. I'll give the controls back to the captain and go myself."

Chris started to protest but thought better of it. He acknowledged the message on the screen and went back to warn the passengers about the fighter's arrival, while Zane gave control of the ship back to the captain. He climbed up a ladder into the air lock above the cockpit to find an environment suit.

Perimeter One Control was tense with expectation. The fighter had entered the accelerator, but nothing had been heard since. Nathan stood beside the comm chief, listening. Suddenly, the silence was broken as a voice came over the speaker.

"This is accelerator control. We have a fix on the fighter."

Dr. Shaw backed away from the group near the comm console, quietly reached into his pocket and pulled out a communicator. He opened a channel and set it on a table beside the comm console, then rejoined the group.

"He's matched speed with the barge and is closing."

Jerry brought the fighter in slowly, trying to come in above the rear of the barge. The electromagnetic turbulence was making it difficult to control his ship, but he'd landed under worse conditions.

Somewhere in the depths of the station, a lone figure listened to the report from accelerator control coming over the channel from Dr. Shaw's open communicator. He removed a small metal box from his pocket with a flashing red light and a single switch. The man holding the box counted to three, then threw the switch.

The small device mounted on the side of Jerry's ship detonated, and the explosion blew a hole in his port engine.

"I've had a blowout! Losing lateral stabilizers . . ."

The fighter began drifting out of position into a roll. Jerry knew he had precious few seconds before he collided with one of the rings. He did a partial shutdown on his port engine, throttled up, and pulled hard on the stick. The fighter slowly came out of its roll, but he was out of position behind the barge.

The fighter was shaking badly, swinging as much as ten meters from side to side. Jerry grabbed the stick with both hands and dropped down behind the main thrusters for the barge. He didn't like staring engines in the face like this, but he found what he was looking for: Calm.

The electromagnetic currents in the accelerator behaved at least partly like air currents, creating a dead space immediately behind the barge. Jerry completed the shutdown of his port engine and took several deep breaths. He could feel the beads of sweat on his upper lip. This was not going to be as easy as he thought.

His best chance was to blast upward through the worst of the turbulence. Not an easy maneuver, even with a fully functional ship. If he could position the ship just above the slip stream, a landing on the barge might be possible.

Jerry held his breath and pulled back on the stick. The fighter rose up quickly, shook violently for a moment, and then stabilized. Trying to ignore the rings blazing past only a few feet from his face, he scanned the rear of the barge.

He brought the fighter in at an angle, nose 30 degrees off center, trying to pinpoint a relatively flat section at the rear of the barge. The turbulence was buffeting the ship, but he inched her down until the landing gear bounced off the hull. He dropped down again, bounced once, twice, and activated the hydraulic cleats. Large claws came out of the landing gear, cutting into the outer hull and locking the fighter in place. Jerry shut down his starboard engine and breathed a long sigh of relief.

He doublechecked to make sure the seal on his environment suit was good, braced himself for the impact, then opened the canopy. Even as the barge hurtled through the accelerator, he climbed from the fighter onto the barge to survey the damage. The hole in his port side engine was not very large, but the shreds of metal around the edges turned inward. The explosion had come from the outside.

Jerry had no time to speculate further, for Zane had emerged from a hatch near the front of the ship. Zane secured one end of a line to the hull and the other end to his suit. Magnets in the boots allowed him to walk the length of the barge. Were it not for the rings rushing past, the maneuver would have been entirely routine.

By the time he reached the fighter, Jerry was already unpacking the shielding. The roll was quite large and would have been impossible for ten men to lift in normal gravity. Together they unfolded the roll of reflective material and anchored one edge to the rear of the barge using bolt setters. With the edge secure, they rolled the material toward the front of the barge.

They were halfway up the hull when an energy arc hit just ahead. The impact dislodged Zane and he began floating away from the barge toward the passing rings. He thrashed about wildly, trying to grab anything to stop himself. Jerry nearly came loose as well, and watched helplessly as Zane drifted outward.

Inside the barge, another explosion and shower of metal had rocked the passenger section. The new breach was quickly plugged, but this time, the injuries were more serious, and there was structural damage to one of the main supports. Passengers not among the wounded quickly went to the aid of their injured comrades.

Outside, Jerry recovered his balance and moved as fast as he could toward Zane's rope. The rope kept floating maddeningly out of reach. Zane pulled frantically, trying to take up the slack.

Inside the barge, Millie came from the rear to check on her children and noticed that some of the people who had been tended to after the first breach now had the opportunity to return the favor. Ryan and Amie were unharmed.

Jerry moved fast toward the front, checking his tool belt as he loped along. The only thing of any use at all was a metal hook. He jerked it off his belt, stretched as far as he could, and managed to snag the rope. In a flash of insight, he tucked the rope under his arm and ran in the direction of the fighter. The closer he came to the back of the barge, the closer Zane floated down to the barge. By the time he reached the fighter, Zane was back on the hull. The copilot waved a quick "thank you," caught his breath, and then resumed his work.

When Zane and Jerry reached the front of the barge, Jerry handed his companion a pair of cutters so they could cut holes in the shielding for the front windows. Just then, another energy arc hit, this time behind them. The arc hit the shielding and bounced harmlessly off the hull. Jerry gave Zane the thumbs up, and they began cutting.

Chris watched their progress with interest from the cockpit, secretly wishing he could join them. After what seemed like only a few minutes, the two suited figures had finished covering the front and moved on to the underside of the barge.

Chris got up to stretch his legs and walked back to the passenger cabin. The sight that met his eyes was a sobering one. The cabin looked like a hospital ward. The wounded were everywhere, stretched across seats, wrapped in makeshift bandages. One or two of the older passengers had broken arms secured by splints.

Chris noticed the places where the arcs had come through. Both holes were plugged with what had once been seat cushions, but now looked more like big red wads of chewing gum. Under different circumstances, the sight would have been humorous.

The shielding of the barge was completed without further incident, and it was with considerable relief that the two men climbed down into the air lock over the cockpit. In the pressurized room, they removed their helmets and saw each other's faces for the first time. Zane smiled first.

"Thanks for saving my life back there."

Jerry whacked him playfully on the shoulder. "Next time, if you want to take a break, just tell me."

They took off their suits, opened the hatch in the floor, and dropped into the cockpit. Chris looked up from the computer.

"Jerry!"

"Hey, preppie. I see you're still making a hobby out of bothering command crews."

Zane was puzzled. "You two know each other? And what's a preppie?"

Jerry found an available seat and sat down. "We met on a freighter. And 'preppie' is an old colloquial expression meaning 'academy brat.'"

Everyone laughed except the captain, who growled, "I hate to break up such a touching reunion, but I think I'm losing thruster control. I can't stay on course."

Jerry looked over the captain's shoulder, as Zane resumed his position in the copilot seat. A quick crosscheck showed that the thrusters were working perfectly. Zane told Chris to ask the station what the problem was and what to do about it. Two minutes later they had their answer.

"As the rings get smaller, the electromagnetic fields get stronger, creating currents like water in a pipe. Since we don't have any forward thrust, it's going to get harder and harder to steer."

"Great. Why don't we just blow the thing up and be done with it." Zane was getting tired.

Chris looked at Jerry. "You didn't bring any injectors with you, by any chance?"

Jerry shook his head. "Sorry. Only the ones on the fighter. And I don't think they'd fit."

Zane turned and put a hand on Jerry's shoulder. "Listen, you've done all you can here. Why don't you take off while you still have some space to do it?"

"I'm not going to just blast out of here while you're still in trouble. Besides, I've only got one engine working."

Chris stood up. "Wait a second. The fighter."

"What about it?"

"That's our forward thrust."

Comprehension crept into Jerry's face, and he frowned. "What would we do for thruster control?"

94

Now it was Chris's turn to frown. "Hmm. What about patching it into the barge's thruster control?"

Zane laughed. "Not in a hundred years."

"You have a schematic for the electrical patch bay. I saw it in the engine room."

"You gotta be kidding."

"Not at all. We could put on environment suits, punch a hole in the hull, and wire the thruster control from the fighter. . . ."

Jerry held up his hand. "Whoa, buckaroo. Why don't I just climb on board and do it manually?"

Chris blushed. "Or we could do that."

"I don't know how long the cleats will hold, so I'll have to use the afterburners on a timed delay. Do you have anything to drink?"

Zane opened the door to the passenger cabin. "Follow me."

Chris sat down at the computer console and informed the station of their intention to use the fighter as a booster rocket. Several minutes passed before a message came through saying that it sounded like the best plan under the circumstances. Jerry came back into the cockpit looking refreshed.

"I'm off," he said as he started up the ladder.

"Don't try any fancy moves."

"Just don't scrape me off and I'll do fine. If all goes well, I'll see you in ten minutes."

Jerry climbed up into the air lock and closed the hatch. He donned his environment suit and secured the helmet. With the air lock depressurized, he climbed out onto the hull. The rings were frighteningly close.

He grabbed Zane's rope, still attached near the hatch, and fastened the end to his suit. He was moving as fast as he could toward the back of the barge, but it was still slow going. Finally he scaled the small ladder to the cockpit and leaned inside.

Straining over the edge, he carefully keyed in the launch sequence, primed the afterburners, and set them for a twenty-second delay. He knew that didn't give him much time, but the way the barge was weaving back and forth, there was little time left.

He punched in the ignition timer and scrambled down the ladder. Grabbing the rope with both hands, he began loping up the barge, pulling himself along as fast as he could. He was halfway to the front when the fighter's engines flamed on. The barge lurched slightly under him, and it became harder to pull on the rope, but he could still manage. He was glad the barge was heavy.

In the cockpit, the captain felt the surge of speed and immediately noticed the controls handling better. "That's more like it." He looked off into the distance and saw something to make even his crusty old heart sing. "Look!"

Chris looked. The end was in sight.

Zane came through the door. "Did he do it already?"

Chris tried not to sound worried. "Yeah. He should be back any minute."

Jerry was thirty feet from the hatch. He felt the hull shudder under his feet and looked back, watching in horror as the cleats from the fighter pulled up a section of the hull. The ceiling of the engine room came with it, along with the electrical relay panel.

Inside the barge, the lights went out and the captain lost thruster control. Some of the passengers still had energy to scream, but most of them simply sat, waiting grimly.

The fighter finally tore loose and careened up the barge toward Jerry. The doomed craft bounced off the hull and flew overhead, slamming into the second ring from the end of the accelerator. Fighter and ring exploded, touching off the explosion of the last ring. Debris showered on the barge and Jerry's body bounced off the hull and into space.

The barge catapulted out the end of the accelerator in a plume of fire and wreckage, and hurtled toward deep space.

CHAPTER 6

"There's been an explosion." The communications chief could hardly believe he was saying it.

"What caused it?" Nathan asked, afraid of the answer.

An officer at another console spoke up. "I'm tracking a large vessel moving away from the accelerator."

"Then it wasn't the barge."

The comm chief raised his hand for silence. "Accelerator control says they lost two rings."

"Any sign of the fighter?"

"Negative."

Nathan said a quick prayer for Jerry. "See if you can raise them on the communicator."

When the noise and the shaking stopped, an unnatural silence ensued on the barge. Emergency lighting came on in the cockpit and the passenger cabin. Everyone was a bit shaken, but it seemed that there were no further injuries.

Stars drifted past the windows, as the barge tumbled slowly end over end. Zane was semiconscious in the copilot's seat, having been put there moments before by the captain and Chris. He had been standing as the barge neared the end of the accelerator, and when the rings exploded he was thrown to the floor.

The captain returned to the business of trying to restore thruster control.

Realizing that Jerry had never come back, Chris quietly climbed up the ladder into the air lock. He closed the hatch behind him and began putting on Zane's environment suit. He spent a few minutes trying to familiarize himself with the controls before depressurizing the air lock and climbing out onto the hull.

The spinning of the stars made him dizzy, so he concentrated on the hull. There was no sign of Jerry or the fighter. The accelerator was already out of sight as well. He looked around once more and then noticed the rope floating over the edge of the barge.

Chris grabbed the rope and began to walk. The spinning of the barge was pulling him outward, but the magnetic boots were holding. Pipes and conduits lining the hull slowed him down, but at least they provided something to hang on to. He refused to give up hope, but then he saw the end of the rope.

"Oh, no. Please . . ." The end of the rope was torn and frayed. Jerry was gone.

Chris resisted an irrational urge to search the heavens for his friend. Even if Jerry was alive, the chances of him being found before his air ran out were next to zero. He didn't even know if the barge would ever be found. The thought of spending his last hours tumbling through space sent a chill through his bones, and he retraced his steps to the hatch.

Using the rope to pull himself along, he made better time and was soon down the hatch into the air lock. He repressurized the room and took off the environment suit, feeling numb inside. As soon as he dropped into the cockpit, the captain gave him a questioning look.

"He's gone," Chris said woodenly.

"I'm sorry. He was a good man. What's the damage?"

"About half the engine room is gone. No sign of the electrical relay panel."

The captain put his head in his hands.

"How's Zane?" Chris asked, noticing that he could see his breath.

"I think he's going into shock. The temperature's dropping fast."

"The air is getting thin. How much oxygen do we have left?"

"All the filters are out. Probably about two hours."

Chris closed his eyes and ran a hand through his hair. "That doesn't give them much time to find us."

The captain said nothing. He knew the capabilities of the station. No one could even look for them. There would be no rescue.

"Try again." Nathan was leaning over the comm chief.

"With all respect, sir; we've been trying for twenty minutes. If she was able to respond, she would have."

Dr. Shaw put a hand on Nathan's shoulder. "There's nothing we can do."

"I don't agree."

"I need your help, Nathan."

"My help? How?"

"The people in the conference hall are starting to panic. If we don't do something to defuse the situation, we may have a mob at our door. Your family is on the barge, perhaps if you give them a report. . . ."

Nathan thought about it. "I'll do what I can. If you hear anything, anything at all, you call me immediately."

Chris was sitting with his family, trying to keep warm. Ryan and Amie were asleep under one blanket, while Millie was curled up next to her older son trying to share body heat. Chris had put his jacket over his mom, but the temperature was approaching freezing and he knew in an hour or so it wouldn't matter anymore.

Chris started to get the shakes and decided he better keep

moving. Millie offered no protest as he left his seat, rubbed his arms, and then walked up to the cockpit. The captain was leaning back with his hands folded on his chest. Zane was covered with a blanket and sleeping for the moment.

"I don't suppose you have any electrical cable and connectors."

"Why?"

"I thought we might steal power from some of the emergency lights and send a distress signal."

"I doubt it. The only electrical cable was in the engine room."

Chris figured it was worth a try. He opened the hatch in the floor and climbed down onto the walkway across the top of the cargo hold. The air was fresher down here. Of course! The air in the cargo hold wasn't being breathed by the passengers.

When he reached the door of the engine room, a flashing red light reminded him there was no atmosphere on the other side of the door, so he headed back to the cockpit. The captain hadn't moved.

"There's oxygen down there. Do you have any power tools?"

"Sure. In the closet there."

Chris opened a half-closet to the left of the door leading aft and searched through a plastic box full of tools. Finally he emerged with a drill in his hands.

"And what do you intend to do with that?" the captain asked.

"Drill a few holes in the floor."

"Are you crazy?"

"We have to get oxygen into the passenger compartment."

"What's the point? We're all going to freeze to death anyway."

"Don't say that. As long as we're alive, there's still a chance."

Chris climbed down into the cargo hold and picked a spot near the wall to start drilling up through the floor. The shielding wasn't very thick, so it didn't take long to make it through. He turned the drill off, and for just a moment, he thought he heard scratching. The sound stopped as suddenly as it started and he moved on down the wall to drill another hole.

He finished the sixth hole at sixty feet from where he started, and stopped the drill. Again came the scratching sound. Chris turned his head, trying to figure out where it was coming from, but it seemed to be coming from everywhere. The sound stopped again.

"This is getting creepy," Chris said to the semi-darkness.

He was halfway down the opposite side when he heard it again. His eyes were becoming accustomed to the dark, so he pushed off from the wall and floated down to the bottom of the cargo hold.

At the bottom of the hold, the scratching sound was more localized and definitely was metallic in nature. Surely nothing could be alive down here. The scratching stopped, but this time Chris waited until it resumed.

Chris moved slowly down the floor, and then stopped himself. The sound was coming from outside. What could possibly be scratching against the. . . .

Horror, hope, and realization all fought for control of Chris's face, as he pushed off the floor and floated upward. He regained the walkway a few moments later and moved as fast as he could toward the cockpit. Bolting up the ladder, he ignored the captain and climbed into the air lock.

"Where are you going?" the captain asked, more out of boredom than concern.

Chris didn't have time for a discussion. "Out."

He closed the lower hatch, threw on an environment suit, and depressurized the air lock. Climbing out onto the hull, he was careful not to hurry as he grabbed the rope and began working his way over the side of the barge. This was familiar territory now, and he made much better time.

When he reached the end of the rope this time, he let go, crouched low to improve his footing, and trusted his magnetic boots to keep him on the hull. Chris finished his trek down around the underside of the barge. Some seventy feet away, an environment suit was tangled in the external pipes at the back end of the ship. *Jerry.*

Chris moved as fast as he could toward the still form of his friend, hampered by the everpresent risk of losing contact with the hull. The pace was agonizingly slow. He had only one thought on his mind: *Lord, please let him be alive. . . .*

As he came closer, he could see the suit was damaged and streaked with carbon. Some of the hoses and cables were nearly melted, and it looked as if the regulator controls were smashed. What he couldn't see was any sign of life. As the barge rotated, first a glove and then a boot brushed against the hull.

Still conscious just after the explosion, Jerry had managed to grab hold of the pipe and tie off what was left of the rope. Chris carefully untied the rope and secured it to his own waist. Jerry had wedged one of his legs between two pipes, and Chris had to use both hands to pull the leg free. This was extremely dangerous, as any unexpected movement from Jerry could dislodge them both, and they would never make it back to the barge. The leg came free of the pipes suddenly, and Chris's feet floated loose from the hull. Terror clutched his heart, and he twisted madly, just managing to get a hand on one of the pipes. His grip was slipping when the angle of the barge's rotation brought them both back to the hull. If he could have, Chris would have dug his very fingers into the metal hull. It was a minute or so before he was able to release his death grip on the pipe. When the fear had subsided, he tried standing. Feet set securely, Chris began towing his friend back along the hull, grabbing any handhold that was available.

During certain portions of the barge's rotation, he could move freely. So he moved forward, taking a few steps; waiting, taking a few more steps; waiting. After what seemed like hours, he was back on top next to the hatch. Jerry still hadn't moved, and there was no way to check his life signs out here. Chris opened the hatch, pushed Jerry's body down into the air lock, followed him down, and repressurized the compartment.

With the helmet removed, Chris put two fingers against Jerry's neck. After a moment he could feel the unmistakable throbbing of a pulse, weak but steady.

Chris slapped his friend's cheeks gently. They felt too cool to the touch.

"Jerry. Can you hear me? Jerry!"

Jerry's eyes fluttered open after several moments and focused on Chris for just an instant.

"What took you so long?" Jerry whispered, trying to smile. His eyes closed again, and his head fell to one side.

Chris threw open the hatch and yelled down into the cockpit. "Get a doctor up here!"

"Still no answer on any frequency." The comm chief put the headset down and switched to speakers.

Nathan was trying to muster some hope. "Maybe they just lost power." No one in the room believed it, but one or two nodded encouragingly.

Visions of his family flooded his mind, and tears stung his eyes. He slammed his fist down on the console in frustration, thinking, *God! Why did You let this happen?*

Suddenly, the speaker crackled to life. "Station control, this is Perimeter Command squad leader responding to your Code One. Do you copy?"

The comm chief snatched the headset off the console. "PC squad leader, this is station control. What's your complement?"

"One light cruiser with an escort of four fighters. What's the nature of your emergency?"

"We just had eighty tons of barge blast out the far end of the accelerator with two hundred seventy people on board. Can you intercept?"

The squad leader let out a low whistle. "We're on our way."

The four fighters and the cruiser altered their approach vector for the last known position of the barge. It took them only six minutes to pass the far end of the accelerator. Raw energy was pouring out the tattered ends of the cables, all that was left of the last two rings.

"This is squad leader. Search pattern Delta."

The fighters fanned out from the cruiser and were soon out of sight. Developed years ago at Perimeter Command, the Delta search pattern was designed to cover as much area in as little time as possible. Because the pattern was used in emergencies, and time was usually a critical factor, they had a 60 percent success rate—not bad odds, in space.

"This is squad wing. I have one mark at zero-three-five."

The doctor who came forward in response to the captain's request had no medical equipment with him. After a cursory check of Jerry's vital signs, he sat back on his heels.

"He's bleeding internally. May have some broken bones. We have to get him to a medical center soon."

Chris looked somberly at the doctor. "Isn't there anything we can do?"

"Don't move him. At least the suit will keep him warm."

Chris followed the doctor down into the cockpit and found his mother waiting for him.

"What's up?"

Millie looked concerned. "Could you come with me for a minute?"

They walked back into the passenger compartment and stopped about halfway. Millie pointed at the ceiling. Six feet of the hull was rippled with interlaced striations. "What does that look like to you?"

"Classic metal fatigue, but that can't be. Something hit the barge. Hard. Probably the fighter."

Chris stood on the back of one of the seats, then braced one foot on a seat back in the next row for balance. He took a small kit from his pocket, pulled out a tiny measuring device, and placed it over one of the discolorations in the hull. After pressing a button and waiting a moment, he pressed another button, then took the device down and looked at it. Millie did not like the look on her son's face as he climbed down.

Without a word, Chris headed back toward the cockpit, with Millie close behind. Once inside with the door closed, Chris took a deep breath and sighed.

"The stress points are expanding at a rate of point-two-seven micrometers per second."

The captain sat up. "Stress points? What are you talking about?"

"Something hit the barge back there. Probably Jerry's fighter after it tore loose. We have fifteen minutes before the hull blows."

The other ships homed in on squad wing's signal, and a few seconds later they had the barge on their scanners. The cruiser hung back while the fighters went ahead to check it out.

The squad leader surveyed the damage. "Station control, we have intercepted the barge. It's tumbling out of control. Looks like something tore up the aft section pretty good. Most of the engine room's gone. I'm going to get in close and see if there are any signs of life. Okay, I can see into the passenger cabin now. It looks like they're on emergency power, but I can see people moving around in there. They've seen us. Somebody's waving."

Inside the cockpit of the barge, the captain sat staring out the front window, mesmerized by the swirling of the stars. Zane was out cold in the copilot seat, and the others had stopped trying to wake him. Chris came down the ladder from the air lock, after checking Jerry's condition. His friend's pulse was weaker, but it looked as if he would hang on.

Chris had all but given up hope when he heard a commotion from the passenger cabin. He hurried through the door and found a group of eight or ten passengers huddled around one of the viewports, waving frantically. Chris knew that could mean only one thing.

He ran to the nearest window to look out and tears welled up in his eyes. Flashing by at odd angles as the barge tumbled through space were four fighters and a heavy cruiser.

On board the cruiser, the commander was considering his options. The ship was equipped with large steel nets that could be deployed to slow down the barge, but the problem was the barge had enough inertia to jerk all the ships off course. The chance of a collision was very high.

Another option was to land the fighters on the sides of the barge and use them as thrusters. Two dangers there: collision and tearing holes in the hull. That left only one other option.

The IPF Fighters were equipped with harpoons and tow cables for collecting cargo and small ships that were periodically— inadvertently—set adrift in space. Unfortunately, the harpoons and tow cables shared some of the same risks as options one and two. A bad shot with a harpoon could tear into the passenger compartment; or once attached, the cable could whip the fighter around like a rock in a sling. Definite chance of collision.

The commander didn't like having to choose between three bad options, but he knew they didn't have much time. He punched the communicator and quickly shared the choices with the squad leader. The two men had been friends for a long time.

"Is that the best you can do?" the squad leader asked sardonically.

The commander almost smiled. "You know your men better than anyone. It's your call."

The squad leader mulled it over for a moment. The other pilots had heard his conversation, and indecision in an operation like this could be lethal as well.

"This is squad leader. Prepare to deploy harpoons and tow cables."

"This is squad wing. We've never tagged anything this big before, sir."

"No better time to learn. We'll target the cargo hold, just

under the nose. Set two-and-two fifty meters in front of the lateral path of the barge, heading zero-three-five."

The fighters moved into position in front of the barge, two above and two below, waiting until the squad leader got a feel for the rotation of the barge.

Chris watched, fascinated, as the fighters started into their rescue maneuver. Then the initial rush of excitement was quenched by a frightening realization. The fighter pilots couldn't know the extent of the damage. If they tried to tow the barge back to the station, the hull would breach before they ever made it. Without power, the communicator was out and there was no way to warn them.

"Give me a hand!" Chris yelled at the captain. He scrambled up into the air lock, hoping he wasn't too late. Grabbing Jerry by the shoulders, he carefully slipped him down to the captain.

"What are you doing?" the captain asked.

Chris knew he didn't have time to explain and slammed the hatch. He threw on an environment suit, ignoring the usual safety checks, and punched the emergency override for the outside hatch. The hatch flew open, and Chris was blown out into space.

On the bridge of the heavy cruiser, the commander swore.

"Squad leader! Hold your fire! Someone just blew out the access hatch!"

"Is he wearing a suit?"

"This is squad wing. Suit is confirmed."

The commander barked orders to his crew, and the cruiser changed course, closing on the body drifting away from the barge.

The first thing Chris noticed was a sharp hissing coming from the neck of his suit. The helmet seal was bad and he was losing oxygen fast. He watched helplessly as the barge slipped farther and farther away. He shouldn't have skipped the safety checks.

The cruiser came in low over his spinning form, and a wide ramp dropped open at the front. The ramp was usually used for loading equipment on the ground, but the bridge crew of the cruiser had another use in mind. As the cruiser passed over Chris, his body hit the ramp and rolled perfectly into the cruiser's cargo hold.

The ramp closed quickly, and the cargo hold was repressurized. The commander bolted through the door, followed by two soldiers with rifles. They grabbed Chris's helmet and pulled it from the suit. His face was blue.

The commander turned to one of the soldiers. "Oxygen!"

The soldier ran to the wall and pulled an oxygen tank off the wall. Crouched next to Chris, he clamped the mask over his mouth and nose until the color slowly began to return to his face.

The commander ordered the mask removed and moved into Chris's field of vision. "Whatever you came to tell us must be pretty important."

Though his color was returning, Chris was still barely conscious. He tried to gather his thoughts and remember why he was there.

"Well, son? What is it? We haven't got all day."

Chris knew he was holding up something important, but he couldn't remember what. Then the events of the last few hours came back all in a rush, and he grabbed the commander's arm, trying to sit up. "We are ten . . . minutes away from . . . a major hull breach."

The commander pushed him back down gently. "How do you know?"

Chris closed his eyes, struggling to get the words out. "Fighter impacted . . . stress lines expanding. . . ."

The commander grabbed his communicator. "Squad leader! Set harpoon! We gotta get those people out of there!"

The squad leader had been studying the rotation of the barge. "This is squad leader. Even if we do this right, it's going to be a rough ride for the civilians on the barge, so look sharp. Coming up on my mark. Target three meters below the cockpit window in five . . . four . . . three . . . two . . ."

All four of the harpoons shot away toward the barge, trailing their tow cables, and pierced the hull right under the captain's feet. As each harpoon came through, metal fins popped out to secure the target. The shafts of the harpoons expanded, sealing the holes around them, and preventing the atmosphere from escaping.

Now came the hard part. The fighters had to stop the barge's rotation before the cables wrapped around it. The four fighters throttled up and peeled away from the nose of the barge. The cables came taut for just an instant, but the barge kept rotating. The winches on the cables were set just below the test strength, to keep the cables from snapping. With a high-pitched whine, the cables began playing out the back ends of the fighters.

The cables were strong, and the barge stopped spinning and fell in behind the fighters before completing another revolution. Inside the passenger compartment, people who were not belted into their seats went flying everywhere inside the cabin. Those still in their seats tried to help the others, grabbing hold of anything that came within reach.

When the barge stabilized, Millie made sure Ryan and Amie were all right, then ran to the cockpit to check on Chris. The captain's face was pale, and Zane was still unconscious. Then she noticed Jerry stretched out on the floor.

"Where's Chris?" she asked, her fear mounting.

The captain shook his head. "He blew himself out the air lock."

"*What!* Why?"

"I don't know. He pushed this guy down the hatch, slammed it shut, and half a minute later he's gone."

Millie clutched her hands to her chest, agonized by the thought of her son adrift in space. What was he thinking? And why didn't he tell anyone? *Oh, Lord . . . please protect him.*

On board the heavy cruiser, the commander had his hands full. The cruiser came into position above the barge, and the crew rushed to prepare the ship to receive the personnel from the barge. The cargo hold could accommodate the whole lot of them, but the medical center had only a half dozen beds.

The docking tube extended from the underside of the cruiser and sealed over the cockpit hatch. The tube filled with atmosphere, and one of the IPF officers worked his way through to the barge's air lock. He opened the hatch and looked down into the astonished face of the captain.

"Get everybody off! Now!"

The next few minutes were chaotic, as the captain and several of the uninjured passengers herded the others up to the cockpit in single file. Millie had a hand on Ryan and Amie, to be sure they didn't get lost in the confusion. As she reached the front, she saw that Zane and Jerry had already been taken to the cruiser. The captain stood by the ladder, determined to see every last passenger safely off the ship.

Millie sent Ryan up first, then gave Amie a push that sent her floating upward. Millie followed then, eager to put the derelict barge far behind. As she reached the far end of the tube, two pairs of strong hands lifted her up out of the hole. The room was small, barely large enough for the two officers to stand side by side, and she was ushered quickly out of the room by a third man in uniform.

A short walk put her in a large conference room, where she was reunited with Ryan and Amie. Over the next several minutes, people kept filing in one by one. When the room was full, an officer came in and closed the door.

"Sorry for the sudden evacuation. We were told your ship was about to lose atmosphere. It's going to be an uncomfortable ride back to the station, but at least it should be brief."

Shortly after people started arriving on the cruiser, Chris was moved out of the medical center to make room for those in greater need. As he walked down the hall away from the center, he passed two med techs carrying Jerry on a stretcher. He desperately wanted to follow his friend but knew he would only be in the way.

Chris stood with his back against the wall and looked at the ceiling, taking a deep breath. He walked down the hallway, following the trail of civilians until he came to the small room where the two officers were helping people onto the ship. He watched a seemingly endless stream of faces go by, each time hoping the next would be a member of his family.

Four med techs were lined up behind him, so he stepped out of the way to let them do their job. A minute later the stretchers went by with two people he didn't recognize, and then the flow of people stopped. Chris leaned into the room and addressed one of the officers.

"Is that everyone?"

"There's one more. Looks like a tight squeeze."

The captain. Chris peeked down the hole and saw the captain struggling to move through the tube, and then the unthinkable happened. Inside the barge, the damaged section of the ceiling gave way, blowing out into space. Air from the cruiser threw Chris into the two officers, and the captain was sucked back down the tube. Chris lost his balance and pitched head first into the hatchway, grabbing the sides and just barely holding on.

The captain hit the hatch below, but managed to stop his downward momentum with both arms and a leg. Using all of his strength, he pulled his other leg up out of the hole, fighting the terrible rush of air. He knew he would never make it back up the tube.

111

The officers had Chris by the legs and were trying to pull him out of the hole so they could close the hatch when Chris remembered the hatch on the other end.

"The hatch! Close the hatch!" he yelled.

The captain couldn't make out what Chris said over the roar of the wind, but he saw Chris frantically pointing at something. The hatch. The open hatch. The captain grabbed the hatch with both hands and pulled it past equilibrium, and the hatch slammed shut with a resounding clang. The tube echoed for a moment, and then all was silent.

The officers helped Chris out of the room, and a short time later, the captain, too. The captain thanked Chris, and then limped off down the hall with an escort. Chris started down the hallway and opened a door on his right. The room was full of people, but none of the faces were familiar.

About to give up hope, he opened the second door from the end of the hallway. Millie let out a gasp and ran to give him a hug.

"You're alive! How did you get here?"

"They picked me up just after I left."

"After you left! You could have told someone," Millie said reproachfully.

"There wasn't time. I had to tell them about the hull damage."

Millie hugged him again. "Just don't ever do that again."

Back on the station, the jubilation at finding life on the barge had been quickly replaced by earnest preparations to receive the injured passengers. Once word leaked out that the barge was arriving, confusion reigned as everyone in the conference hall rushed to check on the well-being of loved ones.

People crowded the loading area until a large contingent of security officers began forcing people who were not waiting for a family member to clear the area.

Nathan scanned the faces coming from the cruiser, hoping for a sign of his family. Then he saw her. Millie emerged from the access tunnel with Amie and Ryan in tow. They looked a little beat up and exhausted, but otherwise okay. He fought his way through the crowd to meet them.

"Nathan!" Millie ran to greet her husband, with the children close behind, and they spent a few moments trying to hug each other all at once. Then Nathan noticed someone was missing.

"Where's Chris?"

"Inside with Jerry."

Nathan's face brightened. "Then Jerry's all right?"

"No."

Medics came through the access tunnel carrying a body on a stretcher. It was covered with a sheet. Chris followed them out and saw his father. They embraced.

"Is he dead?" Nathan asked gently.

"No, but he's hurt pretty bad. They put the sheet over him to reduce his exposure to the other passengers. There's some concern about infection."

Nathan gathered his family around. "Let's get away from this crowd."

Chris began to protest. "I want to go with Jerry. . . ."

"They'll take good care of him at the medical center. You can visit him later."

The Grahams retired to their quarters for some much needed rest. Once they were in the room with the door shut, they held hands and prayed together, thanking God for bringing them all through safely, and asking that Jerry would be healed of his injuries.

Postcrisis exhaustion set in, and they lay down in their appointed beds, not even bothering to get undressed, and were quickly sound asleep.

Chris woke in the middle of the night, unable to shake the feeling that something was wrong. He'd had a dream. What was it? A mob of people were crowded into a hospital emergency room. Air was escaping through a hole in the ceiling, and in the nearest bed someone was dying. *Jerry.*

Chris rolled out of bed and slipped quietly into his shoes. He left a note on his pillow, in case anyone wondered where he was, and tiptoed out the door. The hallway was dim and cool, and there seemed to be no one around. Pulling out his map, he located the medical center.

The medical center on Perimeter One Station was much better equipped than the one on the cruiser, with a full staff of doctors and nurses and many of the latest medical devices. Chris walked in and stood patiently in front of the night desk. After a few moments, the attendant looked up from his paperwork.

"May I help you?"

"Yes. I've come to check on a friend. His name is Jerry Wysoski."

The attendant typed a string of commands into his terminal and started reading to himself from the screen. He stopped reading after a short time and looked back at Chris reluctantly.

"What is it?" Chris asked.

The attendant hesitated. "He's in a coma. Internal injuries, possibly some brain damage. He's not expected to last the night."

Chris closed his eyes for a moment, wishing the prognosis were better. "Can I see him?"

"Are you family?"

"The closest thing he's got out here."

"Come with me."

The two young men walked down a corridor between two rows of makeshift cots—most of which were occupied by injured passengers from the barge—and through a set of double doors into the Critical Care Unit. The attendant walked to one side and drew back a curtain surrounding one of the beds.

Jerry was hooked up to a heart and lung machine, with tubes in his mouth and nose, and one in his arm. "Here he is," said the attendant in a low voice. "He looks stable for the moment, but if his vitals take a turn for the worse, it's going to get busy in here. You'll have to leave in a hurry."

114

"I understand."

The attendant left, closing the curtain behind him, and Chris walked around to the side of the bed. He had heard that patients in a coma can hear the voices of people around them, even though they can't respond. It sounded crazy, but if there was even a chance he could hear. . . .

"Hi, Jerry. It's Chris. I . . . uh . . . just came by to see how you're doing. I mean, there's a lot of work to do and here you are laying down on the job." Chris searched for a response. Nothing.

"Jerry, you gotta beat this thing. You're not a quitter. I know you quit the IPF, but what happened to you could have happened to anybody. You gotta fight, fight as hard as you can, even though it might be easier to give up."

Chris leaned over his friend's face and stared intently, as if he could make his eyes open by force of will.

"I got good news and bad news, Jerry. Which do you want first? . . . Okay, I'll give you the bad news first. If you don't pull it together soon, you're gonna die. The good news is, you don't have to go it alone. I know freighter pilots aren't much on religion, but you are hardly in a position to enforce your wishes. I'm going to talk about God, Jerry, and I'm going to pray for you. How do you like that? If you want me to shut up, you'll have to make me."

Chris started telling Jerry about the life of Jesus, and the Bible, sharing all the stories he could remember. He talked for what seemed like hours, and when his voice became too hoarse to speak, he prayed silently.

Back in their quarters, Nathan woke up suddenly. Still a little disoriented, he was beset by a strong impression to pray for Jerry. Nathan knew better than to pass it off as coincidence, and he rolled out of bed onto his knees.

In the CCU, still praying, with a hand on Jerry's arm, Chris felt a tingling sensation in the ends of his fingers. The feeling gradually spread until his whole hand felt like it was on fire.

Chris stared at his hand as if it had suddenly become alien to him. On the chance God was up to something, he pressed the affected hand on Jerry's chest and kept it there.

After several minutes, the sensation faded and his hand returned to normal. Weird.

Much later, when he had used up all the ways he could think of to ask God to please save Jerry, Chris put a hand on his friend's shoulder, then left the room.

He could not remember how he got back to his quarters. Exhausted, he climbed into bed.

Chris awoke several hours later to the sound of bacon frying. The smell was delicious and, for a moment, he thought he was in his bed at home. Ryan and Amie were already at the breakfast table, and Millie was puttering around the kitchen. No sign of Dad. "Where'd you get the bacon?" he asked his mom.

"There's a tiny market about two minutes from here," she answered.

He got up, shuffled into the bathroom for a quick shower and then joined his younger siblings at the table, feeling much refreshed.

"Welcome back to the land of the living," Millie said from the kitchen.

"You sure slept a long time," Amie said. Chris didn't answer.

Ryan grinned. "Didn't you know? Slugs hibernate."

Chris made a mental note to whack his brother once he felt better. "Where's Dad?"

Millie began piling strips of bacon on a large plate. "He had some errands to run. He said he'd be back for breakfast."

The family had just started eating when Nathan came through the door. "Hurry up, everyone. We have work to do."

Millie looked up from her plate. "Work? What kind of work?"

"I convinced them to suspend the symposium for two days so people can recuperate. I'm hoping that gives us enough time to solve a couple of mysteries. I wish there were a safe place for you all to hide out until this is over, but there isn't. We can't trust Vick or any of his people, and frankly, I can't do this by myself. I need your help."

Anytime their father talked about solving a mystery, it meant adventure. Everyone hurried through breakfast, but spent time asking God for His protection. Then the Grahams headed toward a small conference room.

"We only have this spot till noon, so let's not waste any time," urged Nathan.

They walked into the room, only to find it already occupied. Zane, swathed in bandages around his head, sat across from Jacob Barber.

"Zane! What are you doing here?" Chris asked, shaking the copilot's hand.

"Your dad told me he'd buy me lunch if I came to a meeting this morning."

Chris looked at the other man, seated across from Zane. "Hello, Jacob."

The round man's face broke into a huge grin and he shook Chris's hand warmly. "Good morning, Chris. I wanted to congratulate you for keeping your head yesterday. Your father told me all about it."

Chris reddened. "It got pretty interesting toward the end."

Nathan had everyone sit down for introductions, but then the door flew open again.

"Hey, preppie."

"Jerry! What are you doing here?" Chris couldn't believe his eyes.

"Well, when I came in last night, the doctor wasn't sure I'd make it through the night. He said I was really busted up inside. But when I woke up this morning, he couldn't find anything wrong."

Zane was concerned. "He should check his instruments. I

saw you yesterday. How can you walk? He really didn't find anything?"

Jerry reached inside his jacket and pulled out two X-rays. "Take a look at these. The first one was taken last night when I was brought in. Broken ribs, punctured lung, internal injuries. Now look at the other one taken this morning. No broken bones. No internal injuries. Just a few scrapes and bruises. He can't figure it out, but one of the attendants told me someone spent most of the night by my bedside." Jerry looked at Chris for a moment, then back at the group. "Whoever it was, I'm grateful. Anyway, to answer your question, Chris—your dad came by this morning to see how I was doing and told me about your little meeting. I thought I might be able to help."

"If you're really feeling well enough, Jerry, you're certainly welcome to join us," Nathan replied, pulling another chair up to the table.

Amie couldn't contain herself. "We prayed for you, Jerry. That's why you got better."

The entire family held their breath, waiting for Jerry's reaction. When he spoke again he sounded subdued. "I had a grandmother who used to pray for me. I thought it was a waste of time. Now I'm not so sure. I appreciate your doing that. Thank you."

Amie beamed.

Nathan stood up. "I asked you all here this morning because I want to know who sabotaged the barge and why."

"Who do you suspect?" Jerry asked.

"Well, we know the Friends of the Galaxy have a presence on the station."

"They've never hit anything this big before," Jerry said, shaking his head.

Nathan sat down again. "True. Maybe the target was a particular person."

"Which makes investigation nearly impossible. Besides, there

118

are so many ways to kill somebody in space, why destroy the barge?"

The conversation trailed off until, at last, Chris broke the silence.

"Maybe the barge wasn't the target."

Nathan's eyes narrowed slightly. "The accelerator? Who would want to blow up. . . ?" He stopped abruptly and began to scribble on a piece of paper. He quit as suddenly as he had started.

"Nathan, what is it?" Jacob asked, somewhat bewildered.

"A list of three suspects. Ares Bouman, Andrews Mader, and Vorvick Shaw."

Jacob was still puzzled. "I understand Bouman and the Friends of the Galaxy wanting to blow it up, but do you really think Andy's capable of it? And Vick! Surely you don't think Dr. Shaw would wipe out the only source of tourism for the station?"

"I helped design the accelerator. My family had reserved seats on the barge the day it was sabotaged. Both Vick and Andy dislike me. In my book, that makes them suspects."

They spent the next hour and a half going around the table, each person sharing anything out of the ordinary that had happened in the last few days. Ryan and Amie talked about the little man, with additional input from Chris. Zane and Chris described the events on the barge and the device used to sabotage the injectors. Jerry mentioned the attack by his former shipmates. When it was Jacob's turn, he apologized profusely, but said that he had noticed nothing unusual in the past few days.

Nathan sat back in his chair. "We need more information. Zane, I realize you need to get back to the barge to supervise repairs, but does anyone else object to being given an assignment?" Nathan's question was followed by silence.

"Good. I don't like the idea of splitting up, but I don't think we have any choice. Everyone watch your back! Your first priority is your own safety. Chris, you and Jerry check what's left of the engine room on the barge. Maybe the saboteur left us a clue. After that, search the freighter. See if you can find anything useful."

"What are we looking for?"

"Anything that might suggest the source of the money Jerry's shipmates talked about. Millie, go to the recreation center and see how far you can get with the station computer. Ryan and Amie, see if you can pick up the trail of our mysterious little man, but if things look dangerous at all, break it off. And stick to crowded hallways. Let's all meet at *The Rosewood* at fifteen hundred hours."

"What are you going to do?" Chris wanted to know.

"Jacob and I are going to have a little talk with Dr. Vorvick Shaw."

Nathan and Jacob Barber walked straight to the control center. When they reached the window nearest the entrance, Nathan knocked on the Plexiglas. The comm chief looked up, smiled, and got up right away to let them in.

"Good morning, Nathan. How are you this morning?"

"Much better than yesterday, thank you, Robert. Is it quiet enough for you?"

"Just the way I like it."

"This is my associate, Jacob Barber. Jacob, this is Robert Meyer, the communications chief." They shook hands.

"We'd like a word with Dr. Shaw, if he's in."

"He's in his office."

"Thanks. And thanks again for all your help yesterday."

"All in the line of duty."

The comm chief returned to his station, and Nathan and Jacob made their way to Dr. Shaw's office. The door was closed, and Jacob was about to knock when Nathan held up his hand. Through the door they could hear voices.

"I'm telling you my people aren't going to pay." The voice was hauntingly familiar to Nathan.

The second voice he recognized immediately as Dr. Shaw. "We had an agreement."

"We don't feel the terms have been met."

"You wanted to make a statement. Here's your chance."

"Do you take me for a fool? I say you blew it and the deal's off."

They heard someone stand up, and fearing they would be caught eavesdropping, Nathan decided it was time to knock. The knock produced interesting results. Dr. Shaw called, "Just a minute," followed by furious rustling and receding footsteps, then silence.

"Come in."

Nathan and Jacob walked into the office, surprised to find only Dr. Shaw.

"Good morning, Nathan. What can I do for you?"

Nathan recovered his composure. "Sorry, Vick. I thought there was someone in here with you."

"No, I was dictating a memo. What do you need?"

"Jacob and I would like a word with you."

"Please sit down."

Nathan sat down next to Jacob and noted that the seat was warm. "Jacob and I had a little spare time on our hands and thought we would try to solve a small mystery."

"And what mystery is that?"

"The disappearance of Dr. Joseph Misenberg."

"I know nothing about it."

"Oh, come on, Vick. Jacob told me you were with him the entire time before he vanished."

"I still know nothing about it. If you've come around here chasing old ghosts, then you'll have to excuse me. I have a lot of work to do."

Nathan stood up and started toward the door, but Jacob

pulled him aside. "You go ahead. I want to talk to him alone. He may say things to me that he wouldn't say to you."

Nathan nodded and walked out the door, closing it behind him.

"You idiot!" Dr. Shaw hissed.

Jacob was apologetic. "I didn't know what else to do. I don't have your gift for stretching the truth." He was too afraid to say *lying*.

"But now Graham thinks I had something to do with Joseph's disappearance."

"He already thought that. And you handled yourself just fine. We're no worse off than we were before."

"Maybe. But try to keep your mouth shut from now on."

Jacob left quietly. Dr. Shaw stood, locked the door, and then sat back down at his desk. He pulled a detailed map of the station from a drawer and studied it for a few moments. Picking up the communicator from his desk, he dialed a secret number.

"Jacob Barber just became a liability."

Jerry and Chris had arrived on the barge just in time to see a crew put the last touches on some preliminary repairs. The hull had temporary patches, so the passenger compartment and engine room would hold atmosphere.

"This ship has seen better days," Jerry said, perusing the wreckage.

They climbed down into the cargo hold and noticed the harpoons still protruding through the hull. Walking all the way to the engine room, Chris stepped over the faceplate for the injector housing, then peered at the injector again. He was about to reach in to try to free the Y-trigger switch, when he stopped. The saboteur would have had to make the same move.

He pulled a small pouch out of his pocket, removing a little magnifying glass. Slowly, meticulously, he began to examine the perimeter of the injector housing.

"What are you doing?" Jerry wanted to know.

"Looking for—" he stopped and automatically pulled a plastic container and tweezers out of his pouch, "fibers." He plucked some tiny threads from the rough lip of the injector housing, placing them carefully in the plastic container and sealing it.

"Where'd you learn to do that?"

"Growing up with my father." He reached in with a pocket knife and pried what was left of the Y-trigger switch out from behind the injector. He placed that in another plastic container and stuck them both back in his pocket. "Let's go check the freighter."

Jerry shrugged. "You're the detective."

They left the wreck of the barge, both feeling relieved though neither would admit it, and walked several bays down to where the freighter was docked at Docking Bay Number 5. Walking on the freighter brought back very different memories for each of them. Jerry clapped his hand to his forehead.

"Oh, no. I completely forgot about Griff and Sten."

"What about them?"

"I was going to report the . . . um . . . incident when I found out about the barge. It slipped my mind completely."

"Do you want to go report it now?"

"No. Let's see if we can retrieve the bodies."

They sealed the hatch. Jerry walked into the cockpit, went through the pre-launch sequence, and fired up the engines. Chris watched with envy. There was a part of him that had always wanted to be a pilot.

"Station control, this is freighter NK7544 requesting clearance to depart."

"NK7544, this is station control. The flight plan I have logged has you departing yesterday."

"Scrap it. This is just a short search and recovery run."

"Affirmative. Watch the light cruiser docked in your area."

"The PC cruiser and fighters are still here?"

"I have them leaving for Perimeter Command tomorrow at sixteen hundred hours."

Jerry flashed a grin at Chris. He raised the communicator again. "Station control, cancel request for search and recovery and see if you can track down one of those fighter pilots for me."

"You got it."

Jerry shut down the engines, stood up, and faced Chris. "Let's do what we came here to do."

They methodically searched the ship from stem to stern, paying special attention to the crew quarters. When the search produced nothing, they retraced their steps again. Still nothing. Jerry's communicator beeped.

"NK7544, this is PC squad wing. What's the CTO?"

"This is NK7544. About this time yesterday two of my shipmates got blown out into space. No suits. Probable trajectory—" he pulled a special calculator out of his pocket and punched in several numbers, "One-three-seven by two-four-two by zero-nine-five. Speed between one and two miles per hour."

Chris was somewhat taken aback by the dispassionate way these men talked about retrieving corpses from the cold of space, but—he reminded himself—space was harsh and unforgiving, leaving precious little room for gentleness and compassion, and these men lived in it.

"You want me to hook 'em for you?" the squad wing asked.

"Unless you got something better to do."

"Dead on target, pack rat. We got some lethal boredom up here. This oughta be worth a few grins. I haven't fetched a stiff since I made sergeant."

Chris grimaced at that. "Why did he call you *pack rat?*"

"'Cause I'm a freighter pilot."

"I get it. It's a colloquial expression meaning 'cargo brat.'"

Jerry snorted into the communicator but quickly regained his composure. "Save your afterburners. You got my number."

"No problem. Squad wing off out."

Jerry stowed the communicator on his belt, and then laughed

at the slightly repulsed expression on Chris's face. "No stomach for dead people?"

"Yeah." Chris changed the subject quickly. "What's a CTO?"

"Civilian Task Order. So are we done here or what?"

"We're done."

Jerry opened the hatch and they both walked through the access way onto the station again. They walked through the docking bay and into a passage leading toward the main corridor. Suddenly, there was a peculiar *whoulf* sound from behind them, followed by the shriek of tearing metal.

Air from the main corridor came rushing down the passage, sweeping Jerry and Chris off their feet and whisking them back toward the docking bay. At the end of the passage, an automatic door came down, cutting them off from the docking bay and sending them sprawling on the floor.

Jerry was up first. "You okay?"

Chris lay on the floor nearby, taking inventory. He sat up. "I think so. What was that?"

Jerry's face was ashen. "I think it was the freighter."

CHAPTER 7

Millie Graham had been logged onto the computer for some time, and so far had only managed to turn up page after page of insipid notes and messages from users of the bulletin board system.

The bulletin board system had been set up as a novelty for the guests and a historical record for anyone who was so inclined. Some of the messages on the data base dated all the way back to the opening of the station twenty years before.

All of the official subsystems were classified, which meant she could access only games, the bulletin board, and the electronic shopping mall. All of which were getting her nowhere. Not knowing any of the names of station personnel, she couldn't even search for messages by name.

She decided to try a search by subject. She typed in SHAW and waited while the computer pulled up all messages matching the search string. Only two references turned up, both about an old Earth author.

Frustrated by such a poor return, she typed MISENBERG and hit *Return*. The computer took considerably longer this time and produced over fifteen hundred entries. Millie smiled and cleared the buffer. Then she had another idea. She set it to search by name and typed in MISENBERG.

"NO MESSAGES MATCH YOUR REQUEST."

She typed MIZENBERG.

"NO MESSAGES MATCH YOUR REQUEST."

She began typing variations of the name, changing letters at random, typing faster each time, until her fingers began to miss the right keys. Finally, she typed MISENBVERGF.

"ONE MESSAGE MATCHES YOUR REQUEST."

She suppressed a squeal of delight and selected the *Read* option.

ORIGINATOR: MISENBVERGF, J.
SUBJECT: DRISEN ON THE MISBAND
MESSAGE:
   THE CUSTING OF THE PEISLE AS NEVER BRANDY DOOR FOR. IT SEEMS LIKEN WILL BEEK NAFOOD EETING. DRILLIG WASN TOLDIF MINE WHENS GLRUEN MY BED. STILL, THEN SIG MAFLE BARZ ON THE SIDEL. I WISH THWEULD LTD JE GO BA VK TWIO EIOREK.

She reread the message several times, trying to make sense out of it, before she noticed the date. Her mouth dropped open, and instinctively she looked around to make sure no one was watching her. She selected the print command, and a moment later a piece of paper came out of the printer next to her terminal.

She looked approvingly at the message in crisp black letters, then folded it away into her handbag. After carefully logging off and clearing the screen, she quickly left the recreation center.

Having been assigned the task of finding the little man, Ryan and Amie decided to look for him in the places they had seen him before. They checked the control center first, but found no sign of him and started working their way back to the little alcove on C deck, where they had lost him the first time.

They wandered in and out of side passages, peering into shops and doorways, down stairways, hoping they might get lucky. They were looking so intently for the little man that neither one of them noticed the larger man who was following them, stopping every so often to speak into a communicator.

They arrived at the alcove well after noon, feeling more than a little discouraged. Ryan checked along the wall for any sign of a moving panel but found nothing. He stepped out into the corridor and looked both ways, while Amie doublechecked the alcove walls. She turned away from the back wall and was immediately grabbed from behind by a pair of strong arms.

Out in the corridor, Ryan thought he spotted somebody small enough to be their man and took a few steps in that direction. But then he heard the muffled scream and ran back into the alcove. Amie was gone.

Chris and Jerry arrived at *The Rosewood* early and reserved a large table. Having spent the last hour and a half explaining to station security that they had nothing to do with the destruction of the freighter, they were ready for a break.

Chris put his face in his hands. "I can't believe this. Do I look like a terrorist to you?"

"Well, if I half close my eyes. . . ."

"Hilarious."

Jerry slapped him on the shoulder. "Aw, lighten up. It's not so bad."

"Lighten up? If we'd gone looking for your buddies, we'd be dead right now."

"True. I'm glad no one was on the ship when it blew, but I sure would like to know who's trying to kill me."

Chris had a thought. "Wait a minute. Maybe no one is trying to kill you."

"Right. My freighter was a victim of spontaneous combustion."

"No. You said Griff and Sten tried to kill you."

Jerry took a drink from his water glass. "And they nearly succeeded."

"What if they had succeeded?"

"Then I would have been dead yesterday."

"And?"

Jerry thought for a moment. "And the barge probably wouldn't have made it."

"Yeah, yeah. You're a big hero. What about Griff and Sten?"

"They would have . . . they would have . . . taken off in the freighter." Jerry's voice trailed off.

"And two hours later—kaboom."

Jerry's face broke into a grin. "Maybe no one's trying to kill me after all."

Nathan and Jacob came in and sat down at the table, exchanging greetings with the two already seated.

Nathan put a hand on his son's shoulder. "Thank God you're all right." He turned to face Jerry. "I see station security finally turned you loose. I'm sorry about the freighter, but at least you two weren't on board."

"How was your meeting with Dr. Shaw?" Jerry asked.

"Brief. I'm afraid neither Jacob nor I had any luck getting information out of him. We spent the rest of the time interviewing station personnel. Either nobody knows anything, or Dr. Shaw has them all under his thumb. Did you two turn up anything?"

Chris pulled the plastic containers out of his pocket. "I found some fibers on the edge of the injector housing on the barge. The other container is what's left of the Y-trigger switch. Also, we think whoever blew up the freighter was aiming for Jerry's shipmates."

"What makes you think that?"

"Well, if those two had managed to kill Jerry, they would have taken off right away. My guess is that the timer on the explosive was triggered by starting the engines."

"Interesting. But we still need a motive," Nathan mused.

Millie walked in just then and sat down next to her husband, looking a little smug. "Well? Aren't you going to ask me if I found anything?"

Nathan smiled. "Dear, did you find anything?"

She reached into her handbag and produced the message she

had printed earlier. Her husband unfolded it and read silently.

"What is it?" Chris wanted to know.

"Assuming it's authentic, and the name is a typo, it looks like it could be either a coded message or a garbled one from Joseph Misenberg."

Millie reached over and pointed to the bottom of the page. "Look at the date."

Nathan's eyebrows went up. "Dated six months after his disappearance."

He was about to hand the note to Chris, when Ryan came running in, out of breath.

"They got Amie."

As soon as Ryan had explained how Amie disappeared, Chris pulled out his map of the station, laying it out on the table top.

He looked steadily at Ryan, trying to stay calm. "Show me where the alcove is."

Ryan looked at the map for a moment. "Right there."

"I knew it! I can't believe I didn't see it before."

"What is it, Chris?" Nathan came over from the other side of the table to look, and everyone gathered around.

"See this area behind the alcove wall? It shows solid, but if it really were, the specific weight would send it crashing down two decks and through the wall of the station."

Nathan scribbled some computations on a napkin. "You're right, assuming it's all the same material."

Millie was frantic. "But what about *Amie?*"

"She's in there somewhere. It has to be hollow, Dad. And there are areas just like this all over the map." Chris pointed out several.

Nathan stood up. "Jacob and I will go and report this to station security."

Chris did not think this was a good idea. "What if they're in on it?"

"They would still expect us to report it. For now, we don't

want to arouse any suspicions. Chris, you and Ryan escort your mother back to the room. If Amie escapes, that's the first place she'll try to find us. Go on, Millie—we'll find her," he said to his wife reassuringly.

The two groups split up, leaving Jerry at the table by himself. He looked thoughtfully down at his communicator and played with the buttons. When the waiter came up with the bill for their untouched drinks, Jerry smiled ironically and paid him.

After Amie had been pulled through the opening in the wall, she found herself in a dimly lit passageway inside the walls. The door closed impossibly fast, shutting off the light from the alcove, and she was dragged brusquely down the dark passage.

As the initial terror subsided, she began to struggle, trying to leave as much of a trail as possible. She saw a side passage going by and stuck her leg out, whacking it on the corner as she was dragged past. Pain shot through her shin, and her assailant jerked her around so she was in front of him.

"Stop struggling," he growled menacingly.

Amie stopped struggling. He threw her over his shoulder in a fireman's carry and headed down the passage again.

Millie and her two boys walked into the passenger section of C deck, headed for their room. Ryan saw him first. His mouth dropped open, but no sound came out as he saw the little man right outside their door.

"It's him!" he finally yelled.

Chris took off like a shot, and as the little man turned to run, he hit him with a flying tackle. They rolled and came up with Chris on top. He grabbed the man by the collar.

"Who are you and what have you done with my sister?"

"I'm Lynch Kalland and I didn't do anything to your sister!"

Millie walked up cautiously "Lynch?"

"Yes, Millie. It's me."

"What are you . . . why are you . . . ," Millie sputtered helplessly.

"If you'll get your son off me, I will be happy to answer all of your questions."

Chris got up and offered his hand to Lynch, who gratefully accepted it. They went into the room and settled down in the dining chairs. Millie made Lynch a cup of coffee as her sons watched incredulously.

"Chris, Ryan, this is Lynch Kalland. He was on the same design team with your father twenty-five years ago." Millie peered uneasily at the little man sitting across from her. "Lynch, do you know anything about my daughter? She's missing."

"I was afraid something like this would happen."

"Then you don't know where she is?"

"Not exactly. There are hidden passages all over the station. They were originally intended for maintenance, but Vick had them erased from all the schematics."

"How is Dr. Shaw mixed up in this?" Chris asked quickly.

"I work for him as chief of security. He lobbied hard to get the symposium held on the station, after he saw the guest list. When I saw your names on the list, I was afraid he was going to hurt Nathan. That's why I left that message telling you to leave."

Millie was puzzled. "*You* wrote that message? Why didn't you just talk to us?"

"Vick has eyes everywhere. I couldn't risk it. When you decided to stay, I tried to keep track of your children in case Vick went after them, but that didn't work so well. Then today I overheard some of those FOG people talking about taking the girl. I was coming to find you when you . . . er . . . found me." Lynch looked at Chris reproachfully.

Millie was trying hard to understand. "Why take Amie?"

"Vick wants to hurt Nathan. He holds him responsible for Vick's losing the accelerator project. I haven't figured out how, but I think he had something to do with that barge business."

"Will he hurt Amie?"

"I don't think so. Not yet, anyway."

Jerry walked down the ramp into the security shuttle bay. Three fighters were parked in the bay, fueled up and ready to go. One of the pilots was up on a ladder, leaning into his cockpit. He was a dark-haired, well-muscled man in his early thirties.

Jerry walked to the foot of the ladder. "Excuse me."

The pilot looked down. "What can I do for you?"

"I called in the CTO to hook the stiffs."

The pilot smiled broadly and climbed down the ladder extending his hand. "Charmed. Squad wing sailed minus forty. Minus ten he says he has Tweedledum. Tweedledee in plus fifteen."

Jerry's reply was cut off by a finger poking him in the shoulder. He turned to find one of the station pilots standing behind him, his round face very red.

"You got a lot of nerve showing up here after what you did to our fighter."

The pilot flashed Jerry an interested look. "You're the guy who tagged the barge?"

Jerry nodded.

The pilot looked hard at the angry round face across from him. "Lighten up, porky. He's a friend of mine."

The station pilot took one look at the tightly muscled torso of the fighter pilot and abruptly lost his indignation. He turned without a word and shuffled back to his office.

Jerry smiled. "Thanks."

"Hey, no problem." The pilot put his arm around Jerry's shoulder. "Listen, I got a bet with squad wing that you used a time delay on your afterburners. . . ."

Nathan and Jacob had no luck with station security. They wanted forms filled out and endless approvals before they would do anything.

The two men left in disgust and returned to the Grahams's

133

quarters. They had quite a surprise when they found Lynch Kalland, and an even bigger one when they discovered he was the little man who had been following Amie and Ryan. After some vigorous handshaking, they listened with interest to his whole story.

When Lynch reached the end, Nathan sat back and tried to take it all in. The big picture was getting clearer, but there were still some pieces missing.

"It's getting pretty late in the day. Anyone who can sleep should do so," Nathan suggested. "I'm going to try to come up with a plan."

Jacob and Lynch stood up, preparing to take their leave. Nathan turned toward them. "I think you two should stay here for the night."

Jacob started to protest. "I'm not much good at strategy, and I'm exhausted. . . ."

"Relax, Jacob. You can sleep here. We already know the person, or persons, we are up against are capable of murder. We have an extra bed, and one of you can sleep on the floor."

The two guests reluctantly agreed, and Millie went to work on dinner. Nathan could tell by the look on her face that something was terribly wrong. He came up beside her in the kitchen and spoke softly, so no one could hear.

"I know you want to go out right now and try to save Amie, but it's me they're after. If their plan was to kill her, they wouldn't have taken her alive. We need a little time to come up with a plan."

Millie didn't look up. "I know you're doing what you think is right. I just can't stand the thought of sitting around here while she's in trouble."

Nathan put his arm around her. "Don't worry. We'll put this time to good use. This is one plan that must not fail."

While Millie, Jacob, and Ryan got ready for bed, Nathan, Lynch, and Chris sat down at the kitchen table and studied the map.

"They could be keeping her anywhere," Chris said.

Nathan nodded. "They didn't get Ryan, so they probably know we have a good idea where they grabbed her. They would try to put some distance between that spot and their hideout. Lynch, any ideas?"

"Chris is right. The superstructure is heavily interlaced with maintenance tunnels. They could be keeping her anywhere."

Nathan rested his head on his palm for a moment, thinking. "Is there anything in the control center that might help us find her?"

"Oh! Of course! I mean, yes and no." Lynch paused for a moment trying to pull his thoughts together.

Nathan was understandably impatient. "What are you talking about?"

"When Ryan and Amie were in the low-gravity gymnasium, I placed a couple of small tracking devices on their clothing. The monitor is in my office in the control center. The problem is, at this point I wouldn't be surprised to find that Vick suspects my involvement. I don't mind being in danger, but you really can't afford to lose me right now."

'You got that right," Nathan agreed, patting his old friend on the shoulder.

Chris was curious. "What did the devices look like?"

"Small disks about the size of a fingernail. Hold on a minute, I'll show you."

Lynch walked over to Ryan's bed and picked up a pair of tennis shoes. After looking at them closely, he used tweezers to remove a small device, and returned to the table.

"That's a standard transponder," Chris said, after a brief examination.

"That was all I needed. It worked fine for a while."

"Where's the one you put on Amie?"

"In one of her barrettes."

"And they're set to the same frequency?"

"Yes."

Chris picked up the transponder to examine it more closely. "If we can rewire this thing, we could use it to find Amie."

Lynch looked skeptical. "Your range would be limited."

"Yeah, but at least we'd know when we were close."

Nathan held up a hand to interrupt. "Those things have sub-micron circuitry. We don't have the tools to make modifications."

In response, Chris just smiled and walked over to a dresser set into the wall. Opening the bottom drawer, he moved aside some shirts and pulled out a carrying case, slightly smaller than a briefcase. He set the case on the table and opened it. Inside was a control panel, a tool kit, and a few other items not immediately identifiable.

"What is that?" Nathan asked.

"MRV."

"Merv?"

"MRV. It stands for microscopic remote vehicle."

Without another word, Chris rummaged through his tool kit for a tiny monitor and control panel, then started preparing the MRV for its journey into the transponder.

For Amie, it was a long night. Tied to a chair with cords, she tried in vain to fall asleep. Every time she nodded off, she slumped forward until the pain from the cords awakened her. The room where she was being held was dimly lit, with only one exit. She had tried to move the chair, but it was bolted to the deck. Terror began to well up inside her all over again, but she took several deep breaths and bit her lip to keep from crying.

She decided her only hope was to keep trying to leave a trail. Her hands were tied behind her back, so even if she had had anything in her pockets, she couldn't reach it. Closing her eyes, she mentally looked herself over from head to toe. In her mind's eye, she saw her hair. *The barrettes!*

She began to shake her head, hoping to loosen one of the two plastic clamps. She shook for quite some time, until her neck and head began to ache and she started to feel dizzy.

Finally, one of the barrettes slipped off and fell at her feet. She covered it with her foot and settled in for a long wait.

Sitting alone in the dark, Amie decided that, next to the fear of getting killed, the worst part about being kidnapped was the boredom. She had read articles about hostages who were held for years by their captors. The ones who came through the ordeal in the best shape usually had devoted considerable effort to mental disciplines. She tried to think of something that would provide a suitable amount of distraction, but nothing came to mind. The events of the past few days were fresh, but not the best fodder for meditation, so she thought further back. Nothing.

Amie opened her eyes and stared into the darkness for a moment, comforting herself with the thought that dead ends are a normal part of mental disciplines, or if they weren't, they should be. The effort of thinking was making her tired, but not enough to fall asleep. She wished she had a game, any game, to play. *A game. That's not bad.* She could play an imaginary game of chess . . . she could play an imaginary game of chess with her brother . . . she could play an imaginary game of chess with her brother—and win.

The Graham family and their guests were up early the next day. Plans were finalized quickly over a breakfast of toast and eggs. Jerry showed up at the door a short time later and was invited in for a quick briefing before they headed off for the alcove where Amie had disappeared.

The first stop was Jacob's quarters. He let himself in to pick up a few items but stopped abruptly.

"Nathan!"

Nathan and the others ran inside to see what was the matter. A large hole had been blown through the wall, and Jacob's bed was in pieces on the floor. Nathan looked it over.

"Some kind of explosive device blew this hole in the wall. It looks like the explosion ruptured one of the primary coolant ducts behind the wall. The bed was instantly cooled to minus two hundred twelve degrees Fahrenheit, and it shattered."

Lynch shook his head. "That's impossible. There are safety valves, emergency shutoffs. . . ."

"All of which could have been disabled by someone with the right knowledge and skill," Nathan interrupted. "Somebody wants you dead, Jacob. Any idea who it is?"

Jacob closed his eyes for a moment, trying to control his fear. "I don't have any enemies. I suppose if Dr. Shaw really is trying to destroy you, he might be after me as well."

Nathan looked at Lynch. "More proof that you're at risk as well."

Lynch nodded, and Jacob put a hand on Nathan's shoulder. "Incidentally, thanks for making me stay the night in your quarters."

Nathan smiled and the group moved out into the hallway.

The next stop was the alcove where Amie had disappeared. Lynch walked up to the far wall and when he was within two feet, a panel in the wall slid aside so quickly, it seemed to vanish. Lynch pulled a small metal disk out of his pocket.

"Proximity detector," he explained. He held it away from the opening and the panel slid back into place soundlessly, appearing as if from nowhere.

Nathan was intrigued. "That explains a lot. That's pretty impressive technology."

Lynch looked down at the detector in his hand. "I suppose the designers thought it would be less disruptive to the guests if the maintenance people weren't constantly pulling off access panels. Apparently no one ever thought about the possible misuse of such devices."

Nathan addressed the group. "One more time, here's the plan. Jacob, Lynch, and I will enter here and start looking for Amie. Chris and Ryan, there are ventilation ducts that shadow the maintenance passages. You might be able to get into places we can't. Millie, find Robert Meyer in the control center. He's the communications chief. Tell him what's going on and ask him if he can help. Jerry, I guess you can come with us."

"I got a better idea." Jerry pulled his communicator off his belt and pushed several buttons. Then he handed it to Chris. "Put this on your belt. It's locked open. If you're going to be crawling around in the ventilation, you're going to need both hands." He wished everyone luck, then before anyone could ask where he was going, he was gone.

The group said a prayer that Amie would be found soon and in good health, then split up. Millie headed for the control center, while Chris and Ryan went in search of an inconspicuous ventilation grate. Nathan, Jacob, and Lynch disappeared through the opening in the alcove wall.

Once through the opening and into the dark passage beyond, they had to decide which way to go. Lynch recommended they go left, as the right passage would end in about a hundred feet. They started walking and soon came to the first junction with another passage. Neither direction looked better than the other, and they didn't have time for wrong turns. Nathan pulled out his forensic tool kit and examined the walls. He was about to give up when he found Amie's scuff marks and a few fibers from her pants.

"Good girl, *Liebchen*," he said under his breath, and then addressed the others. "This way."

Amie was awakened from a fitful sleep by rough hands undoing the cords around her wrists.

"What are you doing?" she asked nervously.

"Shut up." It was the man from the previous night.

He untied her ankles, but in the process, discovered the barrette. "Clever. Very clever."

He stuck the barrette in his pocket and grabbed her by the shoulders, pulling her to her feet. At the last moment, she twisted slightly, managing to scrape her leg on the chair. Her captor slapped her hard across the face and pushed her out the door into another passage.

Chris and Ryan found an unlocked maintenance closet and let themselves in. There was nothing of interest on the shelves, but there was a vent high along one wall. They scaled the shelves and quickly pried the grate off. Once both of them were inside the ventilation duct, Ryan replaced the grate to cover their tracks.

As soon as they had their bearings, they crawled in what they hoped was the direction of the alcove. Every thirty feet or so there were grates that allowed them to see down into the passage below. They pressed on as fast as they could without making too much noise, hoping to catch up with their father.

Millie found the entrance to the control center without any problem. She pushed the call button next to the door and waited for someone to answer. When a technician came to the door a few seconds later, she introduced herself and asked to see the communications chief. The technician disappeared and reappeared a minute later.

"The chief is swamped, but he said please come in."

"Thank you," she replied, stepping past him into the control center.

Across the room Robert Meyer was busily directing traffic. Millie waited beside the communications console a full five minutes, trying not to worry about Amie; but channels were so busy the comm chief never got a chance to look up. She stifled a desire to scream, took a deep breath, and decided to poke around a little and see if she could turn up anything useful.

She wandered slowly around the circumference of the control center, admiring the banks of sophisticated machinery, sneaking glances at reports and into trash cans when no one was looking. She had travelled nearly all the way around the room when she came to the door to Dr. Shaw's office. Her knock produced no answer.

She glanced over her shoulder to be certain she was unobserved, put her hand on the knob, and hesitated. If she were caught, she would have a difficult time explaining what she was doing there.

She looked behind her one last time, then opened the door and slipped inside. Administrative documents littered the large desk. She went through them quickly, and finding nothing of interest, turned her attention to the filing cabinet. All the drawers were locked, save one, which she opened. Toward the back she found a thick folder labeled *Symposium* and laid it open on top of the cabinet.

Most of the documents appeared to be correspondence, purchase agreements, and work orders. Then something caught her eye. A quarter of the way through the folder was a list of people who had registered for the symposium, a list with one name circled—Dr. Nathan Graham. A tiny breeze ruffled the papers slightly.

"Find something interesting?"

Millie whirled and found herself face to face with Dr. Shaw. She tried to think of a clever excuse but couldn't make her tongue move. Then she noticed the gun.

A thin smile played across his lips. "Your entire family is becoming quite a nuisance."

Dr. Shaw pushed a button on the communicator on his desk, never taking his eyes off Millie. "Security, this is Shaw. Has Mr. Kalland checked in this morning?"

"No, sir. No one has seen him since yesterday afternoon. He's not responding to his pager."

"I have reason to believe he is partially responsible for the incident with the accelerator. Please instruct your men to detain him if he is found."

Dr. Shaw turned off the communicator and fixed Millie with a steely gaze. "Come with me, please."

He grabbed her by the arm and dragged her toward the back wall. A panel opened to let them pass and then closed smoothly, leaving no sign that they had been in the room.

CHAPTER 8

Nathan was beginning to wonder if they were headed in the wrong direction. They had covered some distance with no sign of his daughter, but he kept his thoughts to himself as they continued their search.

The group came to another junction with a side passage, this time with no clues to help them choose a direction. Nathan felt a twinge of panic but pushed it from his mind, and closed his eyes. "Lord, help," he prayed, "please help."

He opened his eyes and looked down the side passage, which appeared to be completely featureless from his vantage point. He looked down the passage they had been following and thought he saw the faint outline of a doorway along the left wall.

He moved quickly down the hallway and through the doorway, with Lynch and Jacob close behind. The room appeared to be a large maintenance closet with all the fixtures removed except for one chair bolted to the floor.

He pulled out a magnifying glass and a small flashlight and examined the chair from top to bottom, finding tiny cloth fibers stuck to one of the legs. He put one hand on the floor, and the other on the seat.

"It's still warm. I'll bet they kept her here overnight."

Just then, they heard a hushed whisper out in the hallway. "Dad. Dad!"

They went out and looked but could see no one in either direction. The voice came softly one more time, and they looked up to see Chris's face peering down at them through a grate in the ventilation duct. "We're here!"

Nathan waved a greeting. "We're on the right track. Stay close."

They continued on a short distance but stopped abruptly at the sight of two armed guards blocking the passage ahead. Nathan pulled his communicator out and was in the process of warning Chris when a bolt of energy sizzled past his shoulder, igniting a spot on the wall behind him. All three men instinctively hit the deck, lying very still. The guards strained to see into the dimly lit passage but stood their ground.

"Who's there?" one of the guards called. "Identify yourself."

Receiving only silence in return, the guards began firing again. All of the shots passed over their heads, but one came close enough to singe the cloth on Lynch's shoulder.

Nathan lay on the floor for a minute or two, wondering what to do. Then terror clutched his heart as he heard Chris's voice in the passage beyond the guards.

"Freeze, or I'll kill you."

In a corkscrew of motion, both guards turned and fired, bright energy bolts cutting into the darkness.

"Where'd you guys learn to shoot?" Chris's voice taunted from the darkness.

They fired again, using a crisscross pattern, but stopped abruptly as Nathan and his companions hit them from behind. The guns dropped from limp hands, and both guards slumped unconscious to the floor. Jacob and Lynch tied up the guards with their own belts. Nathan examined their faces.

"Dylan Spaulding. He works for Ares Bouman. I don't recognize the other one."

"Jumping them from behind wasn't very sportsmanlike," Jacob said, standing up.

Nathan collected the weapons. "Neither are these."

They moved down the hallway, pausing briefly to thank Chris and Ryan for their assistance, and proceeded on their way. They had gone another hundred feet or so when they came upon a locked door in the right wall.

Nathan turned to Lynch. "What's behind this door?"

"I don't know. I don't ever come down this far."

Nathan walked to the nearest ventilation gate. "Chris? Ryan?"

There was a rustling in the duct overhead, and Chris's face appeared. "Yeah, what is it?"

"We have a locked door about twenty feet back along this wall. Any signal on the transponder?"

Chris pulled the transponder out of his pocket, but the light wasn't flashing. "No signal, but I'll check it out."

Chris squeezed past his younger brother and crawled back fifteen feet to a junction with a duct that ran perpendicular. He crawled in ten feet, peered through a large grate, and let out a low whistle.

"Dad's got to see this."

"What is it?" Ryan asked.

Chris was already working on the grate. "You'll see."

The two boys dropped into the room below and opened the door so their father and his two companions could come inside.

The room was furnished like a small apartment, with a bed against the far wall. In the bed was a skeleton. Chris and Ryan were already standing by the bed. Nathan walked up and carefully pulled the sheet back so he could get a better look at the remains.

He began murmuring to himself. "Human male. Mid to late sixties. Time of death somewhere between fifteen and twenty years ago. No evidence of trauma or a struggle. Probably died of natural causes. Distinguishing characteristics . . . deviated septum . . . arthritis in the right arm and hand . . . class ring. . . ." His voice trailed off.

He looked at Lynch, who had a look of horrified anguish on his face. "It's Joseph. Jacob, what have you done?"

When he noticed the look of consternation on Nathan's face, Jacob pulled him aside and tried to explain. "I wanted to tell you, Nathan, but I couldn't. Vick threatened to kill me."

"Jacob, what are you talking about?"

"About a year and a half after you were reassigned, Dr. Misenberg," he looked sadly at the figure on the bed, "Joseph began to show signs of senility. Because of his success with the accelerator, he was asked to oversee the construction of the station, with the help of Dr. Shaw."

"Vick and Joseph . . . together?"

"The company felt they had been unfair to Vick, punishing him for Andy's mistake, so they gave him another chance. The two of them worked together very closely for several months, but Joseph finally got so bad that work became impossible. We decided to arrange his disappearance."

"*You* did? Why, Jacob?"

"Nathan, you can't know what it was like watching this vital, brilliant man fall to pieces like that. We wanted people to remember him the way he was."

"*Jacob!* People would have understood."

"Don't you think I know now that it was wrong? We were younger—foolish. It seemed like the only decent thing to do at the time."

"Leaving him here alone?"

"Of course not. Our plan was to keep him here for a short time and then transport him to an eldercare facility on Earth. Dr. Shaw assured us that the transport had taken place."

Nathan shook his head in anguish. "When did he tell you this?"

"About four weeks after we confined Joseph."

Nathan pulled a piece of paper out of his pocket, handing it to his friend. "Then how do you explain this?"

Jacob stared blankly for a moment. "What is this?"

"A message, apparently authored by Joseph on the station's bulletin board system six months after he disappeared."

Jacob read the note in disbelief. "Right after we confined him, in one of his lucid moments, Joseph asked me for a computer to help pass the time. Quite a while later Vick had Lynch clear all of his messages. I guess it never occurred to him to check the dates."

Lynch sighed a wretched sigh and looked at the remains of his friend. "Do you think Vick killed Joseph?"

Nathan pursed his lips. "There's no evidence that he did. Maybe he felt somehow responsible and wanted to keep Joseph here. Either way, I'm beginning to think Vick may be insane."

Chris looked intently at his father. "That's all the more reason to find Amie."

The mood turned from somber to urgent. The men gave the boys a boost back up into the ventilation duct and left the room quietly, careful not to disturb anything.

The search party continued at some length, until the passage began to turn downward. At the bottom of the slope was a large door, with no visible controls. Chris reached into his pocket and pulled out the transponder he had modified the night before. A tiny green light was flashing on the front.

"She's inside."

"It may be proximity-activated," said Lynch, coming forward.

Unimpeded by the closed door, Ryan and Chris moved quietly ahead until they could see down into the room below. It appeared to be a small maintenance cargo bay. Against one wall, Amie was lashed to a crate, and in the center of the room stood a man holding a gun, flanked by two henchmen. Chris was about to yell a warning to his dad, but it was too late. The door slid open.

"Welcome, Dr. Graham. I've been expecting you."

Recognition washed across Nathan's face. "Ares Bouman . . . so it *was* your voice I heard in Vick's office the other day."

The man shrugged. "We had business to discuss."

Then Nathan saw his daughter. "Amie! Are you all right?"

Amie nodded weakly, but Bouman's gun kept Nathan from

moving to her side. "I didn't think kidnapping was your style, Bouman."

"Anything with the right price is my style," Bouman sneered, patting a black flight case by his side. "And believe me, this was worth it. But I wouldn't call it kidnapping. Your daughter was just bait for the trap. Please step inside and drop your weapons."

The three men did as they were told. The two men with Bouman picked up the guns. Nathan tried to keep their captor talking. "Did you sabotage the barge?"

"Not at all. I merely supplied the toys to do it."

"Who's paying you, Ares?"

"A good mercenary never divulges the names of his patrons."

"*Mercenary?* So that's what you call yourself."

Bouman's lip curled into a snarl. "Careful, Doctor." His finger tightened slightly on the trigger. With his other hand, he thumbed his communicator. "I have them. You can pick them up at your convenience, as long as it's within the next five minutes."

Up in the ventilation duct, Chris cautiously pulled the medallion out of his pocket. He was reluctant to part with a gift from his sister, but he knew she would understand.

Nathan tried a new tack. "What makes you think you're above the law?"

"The law? The law is worse than useless. I tried it your way, Nathan. You know I did. But like diseased vermin, humanity keeps spilling out into space, poisoning everything it touches."

Just then something came clattering through the ventilation duct. Ares Bouman turned and fired at the duct near the door, cutting it in half. Nathan screamed "No!" and lunged for the weapon, as the duct came crashing down from the ceiling. The falling wreckage struck both of them, and they disappeared in a cloud of debris.

When the noise subsided Jacob and Lynch were struggling with one of the henchmen. The other was out cold, pinned by the fallen duct. Ares Bouman was down on one knee, cradling his arm. He spied one of the laser pistols and reached for it, but Nathan picked it up first. Dazed, Chris and Ryan slowly crawled from the ruin of the ventilation duct. At that moment, the henchman broke free from Lynch and Jacob and ran for the door.

Ares Bouman used the distraction to make his own break for it. Pushing Nathan aside, he ran through the door on the heels of his man. Nathan was not about to let him get away that easily. He tossed his pistol to Lynch.

"You and Jacob stay with Amie!"

Chris tried to stop him. "You're going after him?"

"He's too dangerous. I've got to stop him."

Nathan ran through the door after Bouman. Chris clapped his brother on the shoulder.

"Come on!"

The boys limped across the room after their father, but not before Chris picked up one of the pistols lying on the floor. Lynch and Jacob stood on either side of Amie and untied her. She managed a half-hearted smile. "Boy, am I glad to see you guys."

Ares Bouman passed his man and cut left down a dark passage. "Move it, Dieter!"

Dieter Grüssen was out of breath from his wrestling match with Jacob and Lynch and didn't much like being ordered around as a rule. He had worked with Bouman for many years, but the two had never gotten along.

They ran past a stack of crates, shipping containers, and old compressed gas tanks, and through a huge blast door two feet thick. Ares stopped just beyond the door, listening. Nathan and the boys were pounding down the hall behind them. Bouman knew there was a good chance the Grahams were armed.

"What are we waiting for?" Dieter asked, suddenly panicked.

Bouman ignored his associate, and pulled a small pouch out of his pocket. Reaching inside, he produced a marble-sized wad of grayish clay and stuck it on the floor just beyond the door.

Inside the front pocket of the pouch were several disks a half inch across. He pressed one into the clay and threw a tiny switch with his fingernail. Bouman stowed his pouch and took off down the hall with Dieter close behind, as the explosive detonated. Though the explosion only dented the floor, the concussion was enough to trip the sensors for the blast door. Telescoping in from four sides, the door closed tight, sealing off the passage.

Chris reached the blast door a few moments later and looked in vain for a control panel to open the door. He slammed his hand into it in frustration.

"We almost had him!"

Nathan and Ryan ran up and repeated Chris's search for the controls. "They must be on the other side," Nathan said to himself. Chris was already headed down the hall to look for a parallel passage, when he stopped.

"Dad! Ryan! Come here!"

They joined him by the shipping containers and followed his pointing finger to the compressed gas tanks on the floor.

"We're not finished yet," Chris said through clenched teeth. Ryan found the look of determination on his brother's face frightening.

"What are you thinking?" Nathan asked.

"Give me a hand with this," Chris said, grabbing the end of a large oxygen tank. Nathan grabbed the other end while Ryan hoisted the middle, and they lugged the tank down the hall, laying it next to the blast door.

Nathan looked at Chris. "Wait a minute. The explosion could kill us. We're not thinking. I want him as bad as you do, maybe more, but he isn't worth dying for."

Chris looked a little wild-eyed. "But he's getting away!"

"Then use your head. What's the obstacle?"

Chris found his father's voice calming, which helped him fall into the old pattern of analysis. "Blast doors. But I've never seen 'em closed before."

149

"Neither have I. What conditions normally trigger the mechanism?"

Ryan jumped in. "Fire or explosion."

Nathan nodded. "Good. Now suppose there was a fire, and you needed to get through the doors."

Chris picked up the thought and ran with it. "I'd be on my hands and knees, down where the oxygen is!"

As one man, the Graham men crouched low and examined the door. In the lower right corner was a recessed handle which, due to a trick of the light, was almost invisible from a standing position. Chris turned the handle through several revolutions, and the blast doors began opening. When the space was wide enough to allow them to squeeze through sideways, they moved out.

A short sprint down the hallway beyond brought them to a service elevator. Lighted numbers above the door indicated the elevator was moving upward, toward the inner levels of the station.

Chris stood in front of the control panel beside the door and used his laser pistol to burn a hole in the lock holding the cover in place. Using his pocketknife, he popped open the cover and set it aside.

"You know anything about elevator hardware?" Chris asked, turning to his dad.

Nathan shook his head. "You're the engineer."

Chris shrugged and started jerking cables out of the control panel, until one of the disconnections produced a small shower of sparks and the elevator came to a grinding halt.

On the elevator, Ares thumped the wall with his fist.

"Power failure. Give me a boost."

Dieter folded his hands so Bouman could use them as a step to reach the ceiling. Using the wall for support, he began pulling out panels until he found the emergency hatch. Even twelve levels up, the gravity was less and he was able to pull himself up through the hole with little difficulty.

Dieter came up next, and the two men stood on top of the elevator. The shaft stretched upward out of sight, and a space of six feet separated them from the wall on all sides. A maintenance ladder was bolted to one of the walls and appeared to run the length of the shaft. Bouman looked at his companion and noticed he had his arms wrapped around the elevator cable, his eyes tightly closed.

"What's the matter?"

Dieter wouldn't open his eyes. "I am afraid of heights."

"It worked!" Chris said, clenching his fist.

Nathan clapped him on the shoulder. "Good job! Now we have to find a maintenance tube before they escape up the elevator shaft."

The three of them began hammering on the walls with their fists, looking for a panel that sounded hollow.

"Over here," called Ryan.

Nathan examined the panel. "We should have brought one of Lynch's proximity detectors."

Chris fished a tool out of his kit. "There must be a manual latch."

The tool had a small lip on one end that Chris slid along the left side of the panel from ceiling to floor. He tried the same thing down the right side and stopped halfway when he felt an irregularity in the grooved edge. Wiggling the tool up and down a little, he heard the latch trip and the panel slid into the wall, revealing a vertical maintenance tube with a ladder leading up and down from their location.

Judging from the numbers above the elevator door, he knew they had to reach twelve stories before trying to access the elevator shaft. Chris started climbing, followed by Ryan and his father.

* * *

"Come on! You're acting like a child!" Bouman said from the maintenance ladder.

Dieter was in agony. "I cannot!"

"Fine. I'm leaving. You can stay here if you like."

Bouman started climbing. The thought of being stranded alone surrounded by a chasm, proved to be too much for Dieter. In one frantic surge of motion, he lurched across the open space and grabbed the ladder. His arms were shaking, knuckles white from his death grip on the wrung.

Bouman gave him a look of disgust and continued up the ladder.

Even though they were getting lighter as they climbed, Chris's arms were aching by the time they passed the tenth level. Two more levels, and he opened a door next to the ladder. This one, at least, had a handle.

The Grahams stepped into a dark narrow passage, and automatic lights came on, dimly lighting the hallway. A few feet down, a broad curve in the right-hand wall revealed the location of the elevator shaft. The hatch in the wall was three feet square, two feet off the floor. Chris quietly worked the latch, stuck his head through, and looked up.

The bottom of the elevator was just above his head. Fifty feet farther up, he could see two figures working their way up the ladder. Chris bit his tongue to keep from making noise and charged up the ladder at full speed.

Nathan saw Chris disappear and had a look for himself. He could see Chris closing in on the bottom man and started to call out, but he couldn't risk alerting the two men to their presence. There was nothing else to do but follow.

Chris came up on Dieter, lunged, and wrapped his arms tightly around his legs. Dieter screamed and grabbed one rung with both hands. Bouman looked down and growled at the sight of the Grahams so close behind. Dieter was thrashing, but Chris held firm.

In desperation Bouman stomped his henchman's fingers, hoping he and Chris would fall, taking Nathan and Ryan down with them. Dieter howled in pain and stark terror, let go of the rung, and grabbed onto Bouman's leg instead. The combined weight of Dieter and Chris pulled Bouman away from the ladder, and all three fell.

As Chris started falling, he twisted in midair and threw his arms and legs around two of the elevator cables. He gradually slid to a stop thirty feet down. As Dieter fell past Nathan and Ryan, they reached out awkwardly and managed to get a grip on his clothes, just long enough to slow him down. Dieter grabbed the sides of the ladder and stopped for an instant, but Bouman got a desperate hand on his jacket as he passed, and the two men slid downward.

Approaching the elevator, Bouman saw the impact coming, cut loose, and absorbed the shock with his legs. Dieter wasn't so lucky. He landed in a heap at the bottom of the ladder and didn't get up. Though dazed, Bouman somehow managed to throw himself over the edge and start down the ladder.

Nathan and Ryan hurried down to Chris.

"Are you all right?" Nathan panted.

Chris tossed his dad the laser pistol, trying to ignore the painful raw patches on his face and arms. "I'm fine. Don't let him get away!"

Nathan tucked the pistol in his belt, squeezed past Ryan, and continued downward. Ryan looked at Chris, clinging to the cable like a cat at the top of a tree.

"Would you like a hand?"

This was no time for heroics. "Please."

"I can't come any farther. You'll have to let go," Ryan said.

"I know. Just swing me down and I'll grab the ladder."

Chris pushed off the cable and got a solid grip on his brother's hand. He swung down in an arc and slammed into the ladder, holding on with both arms despite the aching in his ribs. As soon as he was able to move, they started after their father.

Bouman reached the bottom of the shaft, with Nathan gaining on him, and hobbled across the floor and through the maintenance hatch. Nathan slipped through the hatch a few seconds later and followed him down the hallway, gaining another twenty feet on him as Bouman slowed down to work his way through the damaged blast doors. He was headed for the cargo bay.

"Lynch! Jacob! Look out!" called Nathan.

Bouman burst through the doorway, catching Jacob and Lynch off guard. Lynch tried to pull his pistol out of his belt, but Bouman ran past Amie and plowed into the two men, sending them sprawling to the floor. Lynch struggled valiantly, but Bouman was still stronger. He came up with the gun, as Nathan came through the door.

The two men stood ten meters apart, gasping for breath, each with a laser pistol trained at the other's chest. Bouman found his voice first.

"Mexican standoff, Nathan. You kill me, I kill you."

Nathan just nodded. He was exhausted. His lungs burned, and his leg muscles were trembling.

Bouman started moving sideways, slowly, never taking his eyes off Nathan. "All I want to do is get out of here. This has been a bad idea from the start."

"You got that right. This was a very bad idea."

"So? Let's just forget it ever happened. You go your way, I'll go mine. Live, and let live." Bouman made it sound as if he were being generous somehow.

"Live and let live? You tried to kill my family, kidnapped my daughter, and I won't even start on what you've done in the past. Five minutes ago I saw you sacrifice one of your own men without remorse. There's no way I'm going to let you just walk out of here."

Bouman cautiously picked up the black flight case he had

154

abandoned earlier. "The only way you're going to stop me is by pulling that trigger."

Nathan knew if he pulled the trigger, he would be doing it for revenge. For Amie, for his family—for all of Bouman's victims over the years. And he also knew vengeance belongs only to God.

"Drop your gun and put your hands behind your head." The air nearly bristled with the intensity of the emotion in Nathan's voice, as he kept a tight rein on his anger. Bouman took a step backward but said nothing.

"Not just yet, Nathan."

There, at the main door, stood Dr. Shaw with Millie.

Nathan's hand tightened on the gun he was holding. Dr. Shaw looked blandly in his direction. "I don't need to tell you what will happen if I pull the trigger." Nathan dropped his gun.

Bouman relaxed. "Dr. Shaw, your timing is impeccable."

"And yours leaves much to be desired."

"Yes. Well, you got what you wanted," Bouman patted the flight case, "and I got what I wanted. This will keep the organization going for at least six months."

"We're not finished yet. The accelerator was part of the deal."

"We've already been through that. It was one in a million that they made it through in one piece. Just bad luck. Now if you'll excuse me, I'd love to stay and chat, but I have a flight to catch."

Bouman turned for the side exit. As he reached the doorway, Dr. Shaw extended his arm and pulled the trigger. The laser beam hit Bouman square in the back and he spun around, a look of numb disbelief on his face, and then toppled forward onto the deck. Millie and Amie were horror struck, and even Jacob and Lynch couldn't believe what they had just witnessed.

"Vick! You killed him!" Lynch said, staring in shock at the body on the floor.

Dr. Shaw returned his attention to the others. "Just bad luck."

Nathan tried hard to keep his wits about him, ignoring the

155

painful throbbing in his arm. He said a silent prayer of desperation and pushed out a few words. "So what happens now?"

"Now you die."

Nathan felt a little more of his strength returning. "Why kill me? Not because of that business with Andy?"

"Not entirely, no. I'm going to kill you because you killed Joseph. Because you got promoted while I got stuck babysitting tourists on this rotating garbage can. Because you stole the project of a lifetime right out from under me."

"I didn't kill Joseph."

"Yes, you did. You encouraged him to take the accelerator project, pushed him to try to complete it on schedule. He may have died two years after your transfer, but you killed him."

"He wanted to build that accelerator more than anything. I was only trying to help him."

Chris and Ryan had emerged quietly from the hallway, stopping just outside the cargo bay. Chris cupped his hand over his brother's ear.

"Dr. Shaw's got Mom. I think he has a gun. Someone's been shot."

Ryan's eyes were like saucers, but he only nodded.

Dr. Shaw began moving toward the cargo bay doors. "Help him? By feeding his obsession? You knew what that project would do to him." His eyes became distant for a moment, but never lost the glassy sheen of madness. "They should have let me finish."

Chris squeezed his brother's arm, and the two of them burst through the doorway. Dr. Shaw heard them coming and spun around, pushing Millie into Ryan's path. As mother and son collided, Chris came ahead, dodging to one side to avoid the tangled bodies. Dr. Shaw thrust out a leg as he went by, and Chris stumbled, falling at his father's feet.

Millie and Ryan regained their feet. Dr. Shaw took a couple of steps back so he could cover the entire group with his pistol.

"Ah, your brilliant sons have joined us. How nice."

Nathan helped Chris to his feet. "They have nothing to do with this. Let them go."

"Nothing to do? It was your son's meddling that saved the barge."

Dr. Shaw backed up to the controls for the bay doors, and the Grahams gathered around Lynch and Jacob. Nathan was trying to come up with a plan.

"Vick, if you kill us, you'll never get away with it."

"That's the beauty of it. I don't have to get away with it." He began fingering the controls for the bay doors with his free hand.

Nathan held out his hand, fingers spread. "Wait! Don't be a fool. You'll be killed, too."

"I've been half dead for a long time. This will only finish the job."

"At least let my family go. This is just between you and me."

Dr. Shaw was beyond listening. "It's too late. I have to do this."

Dr. Shaw raised his free hand, and everything went into slow motion. Jacob closed his eyes and covered his ears, and Millie grabbed Amie, cradling her head. Dr. Shaw glanced at the controls, even as Nathan, Lynch, Ryan, and Chris all lunged toward him, trying to bridge the impossible distance in time to save their lives. They were still several feet away when Dr. Shaw's fist hit the controls for the explosive override, and the cargo bay doors blew open.

As the smoke cleared, the people in the bay looked incredulously at the sight beyond the doors. Instead of the unforgiving vacuum of space, there stood twenty IPF officers, looking none too happy about the addition of the cargo bay doors to their docking area. Having expected a sudden and violent death, Dr. Shaw was stunned. The two officers nearest the entrance quickly relieved him of the laser pistol and took him into custody.

Jacob addressed the soldiers in front. "We need a medic."

Three young men crossed the docking area quickly, tending to Nathan and the injured henchman, who was still pinned under the fallen duct.

Chris looked behind the soldiers and saw a familiar face. "Jerry!"

"Hey, preppie," Jerry called, all grins.

"What are you doing here?"

"We tracked your movements using the open frequency on your communicator. We recorded the whole conversation. We were about to blast our way in when laughing boy here punched out."

"Glad you could make it."

Chris hobbled toward the cruiser, followed by his mother and Amie, and then Ryan. Jacob Barber and Lynch Kalland followed the medic who was helping Nathan, as they moved slowly toward the cruiser. Finally, the last two medics brought the henchman, still unconscious, on a stretcher. The body of Ares Bouman was left where it was, pending the investigation that would be required by both station security and Perimeter Command. There would be Dieter Grüssen to be taken care of, too.

"Who are these guys?" Chris asked, as he came on board.

"This is the cruiser that came along with those fighters. They were all just sitting around wasting taxpayers' money, so I asked 'em if they wanted to play a little game of hide and seek. The good news is, we found you. The bad news is, now you have to buy dinner for all of us."

The officers cheered. Chris started to laugh and noticed quite suddenly that he had a couple of broken ribs.

Inside, as the docking doors of the cruiser sealed behind them, the Grahams gathered together and said a prayer of heartfelt thanksgiving to the Lord for delivering them from the hands of their enemies.

Epilogue

In a plush, quiet lounge not far from the transporters to the loading areas, Chris sat nursing a soda. The strips of adhesive tape on his ribs were hidden under his shirt.

His parents walked into the lounge with Amie and Ryan, looking refreshed and ready to face the day. A subdued Jacob Barber was with them, and they were just finishing up a conversation.

". . . anyway, I appreciate your understanding. I'm terribly embarrassed about the whole thing."

Nathan patted his friend's shoulder. "You know there will be a formal inquiry, based on the evidence that came out at the hearing this morning. Most of the charges will probably end up on Vick's plate, but you could be looking at fines and a suspended sentence."

Jacob nodded. "I understand."

Chris waved at the new arrivals. "Morning."

Nathan replied, "Good morning, Chris. We got your note. I must say, you look better this morning."

Chris smiled. "You, too."

"You smell better, too," Ryan quipped. Chris scored a direct hit to his brother's face with a soggy napkin, but immediately regretted it as a stab of pain shot through his ribs.

"Has Jerry left yet?" Nathan asked.

"He should be along any minute."

"Well, Jacob and I are going to have to take off. The symposium is starting up again this morning. Please express to him again our warmest thanks."

"And give him a big hug from me," Millie added.

"Where are you going?"

"Shopping," Millie replied with a hint of mischief in her eye.

"What about the runts?"

"We're going to hit the low-grav gymnasium again," Amie said, happily. "You should come along."

"If my ribs were in better shape, I'd like that. Thanks for the invite anyway, squirt."

Ryan could hardly contain his anticipation. "It's so cool. The ceilings are twenty feet high, with pads on all the walls. You'd love it."

Chris looked at his younger brother with private menace. "Sounds like a good place to teach a slug some manners." Chris punched him playfully on the shoulder, wincing from the fresh pain the sudden motion produced in his ribs.

Just then, Lynch and Jerry walked up together.

Nathan brightened. "Lynch! Congratulations on your appointment."

"It's only temporary, but thanks. Somebody has to run this place." He turned to Jerry. "I tried to convince this guy to stay on as a pilot, but he's not biting."

Jerry grinned. "Sorry, but I got a date with Perimeter Command. They have an opening in maintenance. It sounds like a job with career potential."

Lynch turned to Nathan. "Nate, they're assembling a team to begin repairs on the accelerator. I was wondering if you might be willing to attend the kick-off meeting this morning."

Nathan clearly liked the idea. "Looks like the symposium will have to resume without me. Take good notes, will you, Jacob?"

"Why do you always want to copy my notes?"

"You take good notes."

Chris got up from his chair. "Dad? Can I ask you a question before you take off?"

"Of course."

"What's going to happen to Dr. Shaw?"

"Well, after taking our statements yesterday, the security chief opened Vick's private files and found a lot of incriminating evidence against him and several of Bouman's people. The fibers you found in the barge engines match the shirt worn by one of Jerry's deceased shipmates—the big fellow. Coincidentally, we found a monetary draft for two hundred thousand credits, signed by Dr. Shaw, in the pocket of that same shirt."

"So Griff sabotaged the barge," muttered Jerry.

"Right. Bouman kidnapped Amie, and we saw him murder one of his own men trying to get away from us. Then Dr. Shaw murdered Bouman in cold blood. I'd say Vick is going to be put away for a very long time."

"What about Dr. Misenberg?"

"I'm convinced he died of natural causes. We'll take his remains back to Earth and give him a funeral and a proper burial."

"Daddy?" It was Amie. "Why did Dr. Shaw turn out the way he did?"

"I'm not sure. My guess is, he never forgave anyone in his life, and it ate him up inside."

Lynch checked the time. "I hate to interrupt, but we need to go."

Nathan looked around the circle of family and friends. He asked the group if they would mind a quick prayer and they all joined hands, even Jerry and Lynch. "Lord, thanks again for healing Jerry. Please keep him safe as he travels. Thanks again for taking such good care of us these past few days. Please make us into everything You've created us to be, to Your glory. In Jesus' name, Amen."

He looked up and extended his hand to Jerry. "Thanks again,

and all the best. The rest of you, go have a ball. I know I'm going to." With that the party broke up, each man headed back to his own duties. Nathan looked as happy as his family had seen him in a long time.

Pensively, Chris watched Jerry striding confidently down the corridor for a moment; then he turned to Ryan. "Well, runt, I may not be able to use the gym, but why don't you show me around the station?"

Ryan jumped out of his seat. "Yeah! Follow me."

They started out of the lounge, and Chris turned back to face Amie. "Come on, squirt. You're invited, too."

Amie grinned and ran after her brothers. Millie smiled and watched them go. Perhaps shopping could wait. She was ready for a few hours of uninterrupted peace and quiet.

An excerpt from *The SHONN Project*, book two of the Perimeter One Adventures series:

Chris looked a little sheepish. "I am working on a special project for Garrett Alger, and I'm hoping I can interest you in giving me some help."

Dr. Jadwin put on his patient look. "What sort of project?"

"Well, that's the sticky part. I'm not allowed to discuss the particulars."

Katie started to interrupt. "You want us to work on a project without knowing what . . . ?"

Chris held up a hand. "I can guarantee you it isn't like anything you've ever done before."

Dr. Jadwin smiled a smile that said "How do you know what I've done?" but said nothing.

Jimbo looked interested. "What can you tell us?"

Chris chose his words carefully. "We would be designing a skeletal chassis for a . . . a humanoid mechanism."

Dr. Jadwin pursed his lips. "What you propose is intriguing, but I'm not entirely sanguine about embarking on a project of this magnitude without more information."

Chris thought for a moment. "Let me speak hypothetically with you for a moment. With a project of the scope I have outlined, what are the most likely possibilities for the end product?"

"I'm not very good at guessing games, I'm afraid. You used the word *humanoid* earlier. Perhaps something more than an android?"

Chris beamed with admiration and closed the subject. "Anyway, I think you begin to see some of the possibilities."

Dr. Jadwin clearly saw some of the possibilities, as evidenced by his brooding expression.